Destructive

Bliss

Destructive Series: Book One

by
ABEL OZUNA

Dedication

This book is for my brother and sister, Brandon and Jasmine. Thank you for being the best brother and sister a guy could ever have. I know that I can always count on you both and I hope you know, I'll always be here for you. I love y'all.

Table of Contents

Sign up for Abel's newsletter for a chance to be the first person to hear the latest and greatest:

http://abelnewsletter.com

Prologue

"Adalyn, honey, please calm down. No one will find us here. Aria's Reckoning will be just as smooth and uneventful as Alexia's was."

Adalyn looked over at her husband, "I hope so. I just can't imagine losing one of our kids. I can't go through the pain of losing a family member again."

Liam walked over to his wife. "I know honey. That was a long time ago. Your sister hasn't been seen in over eight years, and we're a long way from the west coast."

Adalyn nodded. "You're right. Anxiety is just getting the best of me. You definitely know me so well, my love."

Liam embraced his wife and stared out of their kitchen window, fear heavy on his chest.

Violet Whitelace watched the couple from her car. "Ethan, are you ready for this? My foolish sister really thought she could hide from me."

Ethan looked up at his mom. "That's funny. They know I'm a tracker, right?"

Violet glared at her son. "Actually, they do not. No one ever needs to know what your ability is."

Ethan let his head hang low as his mom put her hand on his shoulder, "Now, now my boy. No time to let those pathetic feelings get to you. We need to get you enrolled into your cousin's school tomorrow. The sooner you make your way into her circle, the faster we can get her to join us."

Ethan smiled. "Mother, you know I have no feelings. It's just a bad habit I have to break."

His mother laughed. "That's my boy."

He went on, "I'm sure she'll join us as soon as she realizes how great things are as a Dark."

His mom smiled. "Yes she will. Shall we look for a home in the neighborhood now?"

Ethan exclaimed, "Mother, there is no way in hell you can make me live in a mundane neighborhood! They're filthy and disgusting!"

Violet's silky black hair started swirling and her eyes turned from a Light purple to a deep violet. "Ethan Whitelace, you will not talk to me in that tone! Do not forget who you're speaking to, child. You will do as I say. If I tell you that you'll be sleeping in the same room as a mundane, you will do so."

Ethan started choking and could barely breathe. "Mom—oh—ok—okay!"

Her hair fell back down to her shoulders and her eyes Lightened as she smiled. "Sweet boy, you are so brave...and so stupid."

Ethan was still trying to recover from his mom's invisible chokehold when he screamed out, "Mom, there she is! That's her, isn't it?"

Violet grinned. "Yes. That is most definitely her. She will be a wonderful addition to our family. *He* will be so happy once we have delivered her.

Chapter One

"Aria, your 16th birthday is only a few months away. You know we've got to start preparing you for the Reckoning, right?"

I looked over at my mom. "Yes, mother. It's actually ten months away. I just turned 15, for God's sake!"

My kid brother butted in. "Mom, what exactly do you have to prepare her for? Doesn't she just have to be like, okay I'm staying Light, peace out? Oh, and why do we have to wear those suits? They're so hot and itchy!"

My mom laughed. "Declan, sweetie, one thing at a time. She doesn't just say that. She has a scripture she has to memorize. The Dark and Light Fae have their own scriptures that each one must perform in order to trigger their true nature and powers. The suits are a formality. Fae have worn the Reckoning robes for ages. It is a way we show respect to the elders who fought in the Fae war. And Declan, there will be no 'peacing out' at her Reckoning or yours, got it?"

He gave that malicious smirk he's famous for as Alexia, my older sister, walked in, "*Oh God*. Not the dreaded Reckoning talk, *again*. Let her freak out a little longer, Mom." I nodded with my sister in agreement. Alexia pushed Deck out of her way, "Move it, shrimp. You know this is my chair for breakfast. You sit over there, by Dad. He's the only living thing on this earth that can stand your nasty breath in their face this early."

He pushed her back, "You're like forty. Why are you still living at *my* parent's house?"

I snorted. "Ouch! I think he's trying to call you old."

My dad laughed as he walked into the kitchen, "So forty is old, huh? Looks like your mom and I are pushing ancient then."

He kissed my mom and she poked his side, "Speak for yourself, mister. I was just telling Aria that we will need to begin prepping her for her Reckoning soon."

He nodded. "Yes. The Reckoning—dum dum dum."

I laughed, "My thoughts exactly, Dad."

He poured his coffee as he sat next to Declan and said, "We can talk about it more this evening. I'm taking you all out to dinner."

My mom looked at him. "Oh, sweetie. That is so nice, but I still have so much unpacking to do before I start my new job next week and…"

He cut her off. "Adalyn, unpacking can wait one evening. We're going out to dinner."

Alexia got some toast buttered, picked up her car keys and gave me the "hurry up, let's go before this turns into another family debate" look.

"Alexia, can you drive any slower? I'm really trying to meet Shantel at the school, sometime before lunch?"

She scoffed. "Whatever. I am in a serious tweeting battle with some biatch that's in my Economics class."

After a couple of seconds she looked over at me, "Wait, Aria, are you seriously going to wear that on your first day of high school?"

I looked over at my sister and rolled my eyes, "Alexia, I know it's been a long time since you were in high school, but back off. I didn't make fun of your new extensions, did I? Are you in college or the school for sluts?"

Alexia coughed. "You witch, get out of my car!"

I took my seat belt off, looked over at her with an evil stare and said, "Gladly. Bye hooker—I mean—sis."

"Shantel! Hey, sorry I'm so late. My sister drove like an elderly person who forgot their reading glasses."

My best friend of three years laughed, "Girl, don't worry about it. You got here just in time. Not only are there older guys in high school, but we've got some new class mates to look at, too."

I laughed and continued walking with her towards the cafeteria. "Where do we sit to observe these magnificent creatures you speak of?" Shantel has always been so confident. Her hair is never frizzy and is always the right shade of brown. Her skin is fair and unlike a lot of girls that I've gone to school with, she doesn't ever need to tan. If I were a mundane, these are things that would really make me feel insecure about my own appearance.

Shantel laughed, "Girl, your contacts are the bomb.com. Like, I really need to get mine from your dealer. Didn't you have gray contacts last year?"

I laughed nervously, "Yeah, I still have those. I'm using some blue ones my sister turned me on to. I'm really going for the natural look this year." *She didn't know that my eyes have been changing colors from gray to blue for the past four years.*

She stopped walking, "Let's be real, girls with our color of skin do not naturally look like us. They definitely don't have perfect brown hair and blue eyes." I started to agree with her when I felt like I got tackled by a professional football player. "Oh, hey. I'm sorry. Excuse me." He helped me pick up the contents of my purse from the dirty floor. "Here you go. Sorry about that. My name's Grayson by the way."

I looked into his eyes. "Hey, don't wor-worry about it. I'm Aria."

Shantel was at my side now. "You're Grayson Treble, right?"

He answered her, keeping his eyes on mine. "Yeah. Though, it's pronounced trouble."

Shantel squeezed my arm, "I'm Shantel Parks. This is my best friend, Aria Whitelace."

He shook her hand, and then mine. The second our hands touched, I figured him out. He's a Dark Fae. He's a Dark Fae in a mundane school. He's a Dark Fae, in *my* school.

Chapter Two

"Earth to Aria. Are you okay?" Shantel's waving hand in my face snapped me out of my stare-down with Grayson.

I mumbled, "Oh, sorry." Grayson looked at me with the same, *"oh-my-God-she's-a-Fae"* face.

He let out an awkward laugh. "Excuse me, I better get going. Nice meeting you two. I'll see you two around?"

Shantel smiled. "Sure thing Grayson Treble".

He smiled and walked off with a group of mundane guys. The minute he was out of our sight, Shantel grabbed my arm, "Girl, are you okay? You totally freaked and like, blacked out. I hope you didn't scare him off forever. He's *too* fine!

I let out an obvious fake laugh. "Yeah, sorry about that. He, uh, he looked familiar."

She huffed. "Please do not tell me you know him from elementary and had a crush on him."

I smiled. "No, I definitely didn't. We should get to class, huh?"

"Ugh, I guess. I'm so glad we've got homeroom together. Can you imagine being separated from each other?"

This time, I let out a genuine laugh. "Oh the horror. Please don't rip me away from my friend of three years."

She rolled her eyes. "Ew, don't be so snarky. Okay, I kind of like it but use your hate towards someone else."

I was listening to Shantel ramble on about how she was going to stop smiling to prevent wrinkles as we walked into our homeroom class and a tall, Light-skinned man blocked our entrance into the classroom. "Ladies, welcome to World History. I'm your teacher, Mr. Sulks, and you two are?"

I smiled. "I'm Aria Whitelace, this is Shantel Parks."

He stared down at his clipboard. "Mm hm. Okay Aria, your desk is at the far back, left corner of the room. Ms. Parks, your desk is two desks in front of her." I smiled as Shantel sighed.

We walked towards the back of the classroom when I heard Mr. Sulks welcome the next group of students into the class. "Mmkay. Mr. Treble, your desk is actually right next to Ms. Whitelace over there. Please take your seat and get your syllabus ready."

My heart stopped when Shantel rushed next to me. "Oh my freaking God. Grayson's in our class? And he's sitting next to you? This is like, meant to be."

I let a fake smile shine through my sarcasm. "*Yeah*. This is going to be *great*." I immediately took my seat, got my binder out of my bag and started reading the syllabus.

Grayson was taking his time walking towards the back of the classroom and as he got closer to me, I could smell the sweet cologne he was wearing. I could feel the tension building and growing with every step he took. I felt like I was about to pass out from holding my breath when he sat next to me, and put his bag in the aisle between us. He cleared his throat as he started going over his syllabus and in the background of the class noise I could hear our teacher directing the other students to their desks. Grayson leaned over and whispered, "Hey, uh. Do you think I can borrow a pen?"

As I swallowed my nerves down so I could respond, I stuttered, "Ye-ye-yeah. Sure, here you go." I handed him the pen and again, the minute we touched, there was this burning sensation. I felt as if I were laying out in the sun, warming my entire body with its natural heat. He looked up at me and his eyes flashed a Light violet.

He jumped back into his seat, stared down at his syllabus and mumbled out, "Thanks".

After what seemed like an hour I finally remembered to say,"No problem."

Mr. Sulks started talking and going over the syllabus along with his classroom rules as Grayson reached over the aisle and handed me a crumpled up piece of paper. I opened the paper, keeping my eyes focused on our history teacher so he wouldn't be tempted to come read the note out loud. I looked down at the paper and almost screamed out, *"Are you seriously asking me this in a crumpled note?"* I took a deep breath and read it again for clarity: "You're Light. Aren't you? How are you here, in a mundane school? Your council approved this?"

Annoyed, I responded with, "Why is it any of your business? I'm from a Light family and haven't been through my Reckoning. And for your information, my council always approves us attending mundane schools. We're not show-offs with our powers like your kind. And by kind, I mean Dark. You are, in fact, a Dark Fae. Right? I'm not surprised that your council approved your kind to be in a mundane school. They're very easygoing, huh?" I threw the paper back to his desk and refocused on Mr. Sulks. I heard Grayson giggle as he wrote down his response.

A second later, the piece of paper was back on my desk. "I see you have a personality. That's good. I am definitely Dark. And my council doesn't have to approve me being here. My parents are the Royals."

Chapter Three

He's a Royal? Holy shit. I need to get out of here, stat. "Mr. Sulks, may I have a hall pass to the nurse?"

Mr. Sulks lowered his glasses and looked at me wearily, "Mm hm. Here you go Aria. Straight to the nurse and back, got it missy?" I nodded, gathered my things and sprinted to the front of the classroom.

I ran down the extremely long hall way, dialing my mom's phone number over and over, when I heard, "Aria? Wait! Don't freak out, please."

I turned around, put my phone in my back pocket and screamed out, "You're a Royal! What the hell do you mean, don't freak out?"

He looked down at my shaking hands, "Look, can we talk about this after school? I am a Dark Royal, but it's nothing for you to go crazy over. We're in the same class, in the same mundane school. We need to act cordial to each other for their sakes anyway."

I dropped my bag to the floor. "I-I really can't believe this is happening. I wanted to come to this mundane high school to fit in. To be normal for as long as possible. And then here you are, a freaking Dark Royal!"

He laughed. "You wanted to be normal? You mean you wanted to try to fit in as a mundane? That's hardly going to happen. Have you looked in the mirror lately Aria?"

I scoffed, "Excuse me? What's that supposed to mean?"

He showed off his beautiful smile. "Nothing offensive, if you're taking it that way. I mean, you have the most beautiful, blue-gray eyes I have ever seen. If you haven't been through your Reckoning, you know it's okay if we hang out. I mean, until you choose a side."

I rolled my eyes and picked my bag back up. "Um, thanks. I haven't been through the

Reckoning yet, but I'll be a Light Fae by this time next year, so there's no point in us 'hanging out'." Before he could respond, the bell rang and the mundane students flooded the hallway. Homeroom was over and it was time for second period.

The rest of my day at Shadow Hills High went off without a hitch. I tried to act as normal as possible, but when Shantel invited me over to watch some reality housewives show, I had to decline. She was definitely not happy with me, but I needed to get home and tell my parents exactly what happened today. I looked at my cellphone and saw a message from Alexia, "Hey whore. Sorry I won't be able to pick you up today. My study group is meeting at the coffee-shop right after class and I'll be there until dinner. See you tonight. XOXO." *Great*.

As I started walking away from the school, a silver BMW pulled up next to me, "Hey Aria. Do you need a ride?"

Are you kidding me? "Grayson, I don't need a ride. Please leave me alone. You know we can't talk."

He let out a long sigh. "Aria, please. Let me take you home. You know it's going to rain, right?"

I looked up at the Dark sky. *You've got to be kidding me. Today hates me. The universe is after me.* I looked around as if I had other options and after a couple of seconds I rolled my eyes again and said, "Okay, you can take me home. But you need to drop me off and leave right away. I can't have any of my family members see a Dark Fae dropping me off."

He gave me this half-smile that made my knees go weak. "Deal, now can you get in before the skies drop a tidal wave on us?"

We sat in silence for the first couple of blocks and then he cleared his throat. "So, um, what kind of music do you like? We can listen to anything. You dj."

I mumbled, "I don't really care, anything is fine."

He pulled the car over as the rain started to heavily pour down on us. He unbuckled his seat-belt, "Aria, look. I know you felt what happened when I shook your hand earlier. I've met Light Fae before, and shaken plenty of hands. That has never happened."

I looked back at him, "Well, I felt something. But I've never talked to a Dark Fae before so I'm not sure if it'd happen again."

He put his palm up and signaled for me to put mine up as well. I reluctantly unbuckled my seat-belt, turned towards him and put my palm on his. A second later, the burning sensation was surging through the both of us. We stared at each other as he said, "Leave your hand on mine. Let's see what happens." I nodded. It got hotter and as I started to look closer at our adjacent hands, I saw sparks going up our wrists and after a minute up our arms. The minute they got to our shoulders we both fell apart.

He spoke first. "Whoa. What was that?" I stayed quiet, because to be frank, I wasn't sure what the hell had just happened. His cellphone rang. "What do you want Cayne? Uh huh. Okay. Listen, there's something I need your help with. Can you meet me at our spot in an hour? Don't tell Briar, please. Thanks, bye."

I looked at him. "Who's Cayne?"

He met my eyes. "One of my older brothers. He knows a lot about Fae history and has studied it for as long as I can remember.

I'm going to ask him if he's heard about anything like this before."

I shrieked. "Grayson, you cannot tell anyone about me! We are not friends. We can't be friends."

As I looked into his eyes, he said, "Aria, please? We need to figure this out. I have never heard of anything like this happening before. And I know that you haven't chosen a side, so until you have to, can we at least be acquaintances?"

I stopped looking at him, and looked out my window. "We'll see. For now, can you get me home please?"

Through my peripheral vision, I saw his huge grin as he said, "I'll take that. Let's get you home, kid."

As we started to get closer to my house, my chest started aching. I didn't want to get out of his car. I didn't want to not be next to him. As if he could read my mind, he asked, "What are you doing later tonight?"

I tried not to sound excited, "Um, my dad's taking our family out to dinner to discuss my Reckoning preparation and then I wasn't really going to do much after. I finished my homework during study period."

He let out a small laugh, "How about I pick you up at, let's say, eight? I really would like to see you again this evening."

I didn't want to smile, but I'm sure he could hear the excitement in my response. "Okay. I suppose that'll be fine."

I was about to get out of his car when he grabbed my arm, "Aria, I know you're from a Light Fae family, and I'm from *the* Dark Royal family, but let's try to be—what'd you say earlier? Oh yeah, let's try to be normal. If you don't want anyone to know that we talk, that's okay with me. I can be your Dark little secret."

I smiled at him, kissed his cheek and got out of his car. I walked towards my house and when I looked back at him to wave goodbye, I could see his Light violet eyes glowing through his tinted windows.

Chapter Four

Dinner couldn't go by quick enough. My family and I sat around the table talking about how great our days had been and then my parents brought up the Reckoning ceremonies. I wasn't really paying that much attention to our dinner or conversation because I couldn't get Grayson out of my mind. As we pulled up to the house I saw Grayson's BMW parked in the driveway. *Oh my God. He can't be here!* Declan looked at me, "Aria, who's that? Is that the same guy that dropped you off from school?"

My dad looked at me through his rear view mirror. Alexia hit my arm, "Sis, you didn't tell me that you met a guy. Spill the beans. Who is he? Is he mundane? Oh, if he is, I hope that he is super hot."

My mom laughed. "Can you two leave your sister alone?" In a matter of seconds, the car grew quiet.

I leaned forward. "Mom, Dad, do you think that I can go for a ride with my friend? I'll be home in an hour or so?"

My parents looked at each other and then sighed, "I guess that'll be fine. Make sure you're home before ten, Aria," My dad parked our vehicle in the driveway and I ran out to meet Grayson at his car.

He rolled down his window as I lunged towards his car, "Don't do that!"

He laughed. "Um, is everything okay?"

I snapped at him, "Why are you here already? My parents cannot see you. I thought we talked about this already!"

He smiled. "Relax, kid. They won't be able to see through these windows. And I'm sorry that I'm early. I just couldn't wait another minute to see you again."

My heart melted. "Whatever, let's go." I buckled up and he looked at me with his violet eyes as we drove off.

I cleared my throat. "So, where are you taking me?" I asked, as if it mattered. I really didn't care where we were going.

He smiled. "I'm going to a place by the lake that my brother and I hang out at. It's top secret and if you tell anyone where it is, I may have to kill you."

I laughed. "A hang-out by the lake is top secret? Ooh, how mysterious." As we pulled up to the lake I saw a small convertible car at the edge of the lake. A tall, Light-skinned, brown-haired guy started waving at us.

Grayson got out of the car as his brother opened my door. "Why, hello. I'm Cayne Treble. It's a pleasure to meet you."

I started to blush as I stared into his green eyes. "Hi. I'm Aria, nice to meet you too."

He kissed my hand and said, "Oh, I know who you are. My dear little brother could not stop talking about the Light Fae who nearly set him on fire at school." I'm sure I was blushing again.

Grayson interrupted, "Okay Cayne, no need to get into the details of our conversation. Can we go to our place and talk about what the hell happened with Aria and I today?"

Cayne smiled at me, and then his brother. "Sure. Let me get my things from the car and let's get this show on the road. You two are going to be a little shocked with what I dug up. Oh, and by the way, pun intended." I smiled back at Cayne and followed him and Grayson closer to the lake. We were walking along the edge of the lake for a little while when I noticed that just ahead of us there was big hill filled with different colored flowers.

Grayson looked at me. "Bet you didn't know this was here, huh?"

I looked around. "You're betting that I didn't know this hill was here? Well, um. You win. I didn't know this was here and what's the big deal?"

He stopped walking, "Oh, you'll see why this place is so special to us, jus' wait."

Cayne stepped in front of us, lifted his hands up and I saw his skin and eyes glow a bright purple. "Your brother is an elemental?"

Grayson smiled at me, "Yeah, he can control all of the Earth's elements. He's one of the lucky ones, I guess."

The higher up Cayne's hands went, the brighter his purple aura glowed. The ground beneath our feet slowly started shaking and then as I looked over at the grassy hill, Grayson whispered, "You see that?"

I looked closer as Cayne started lowering his hands and saw a door in the middle of the hill. I whispered, "Wow, what the hell just happened?"

Grayson and Cayne looked at me with matching smiles. "Pretty cool, huh?"

Cayne went on, "I use earth to hide this door for Grayson and I. It's a place we found many years ago, so we've kept it under wraps. My twin, Briar, can be a bit of a jerk so we used to come out here to get away."

I hit Grayson. "You have a brother that's a bigger jerk than you are? That's tough to believe."

Cayne laughed. "Ouch! Gray, I really like this one. Let's go in, it looks like it's about to rain."

As I followed them into the hidden hill I had to ask, "If you're an elemental, can't you just stop the rain?"

As Cayne closed the door behind me, he laughed. "Dang girl, I'm an elemental Fae, not God."

I coughed. "Oh yeah, um. Sorry."

He looked at me. "Ah, how sweet it is to be young and carefree."

Grayson interrupted, "Okay Cayne, can you stop being a distraction and just get to the reason we're here."

Cayne stopped smiling and let sarcasm roll off his tongue, "Oh brother, so testy tonight. Very well then, *master*."

Grayson looked at me, and rolled his eyes, "Excuse my imbecile brother." I laughed.

Cayne pointed at the table, "Let's sit down. There's a lot to cover and we've got what, an hour?" I nodded and took the seat next to Grayson. His brother started talking, "Grayson told me that you had quite the meet-up this morning."

I nodded. "Um, yeah I guess you could say that. It was kind of weird."

Grayson added, "Well, it wasn't exactly weird. It was more like when we touched, our bodies nearly exploded from a fire."

I rolled my eyes, "Okay, it was definitely weird and we definitely did not almost explode."

Cayne laughed, "Well, there are three sides to every story you know. His, yours and the truth." Grayson and I started to giggle and Cayne went on, "I started digging around as soon as my brother called me. I've heard about something similar to this, but it hasn't happened for many, many years."

Grayson pushed his brother on, "Okay, so what is it? Why did we feel a burning sensation when we touched? How did sparks come out from our fingertips?"

Cayne put his books down and looked over at us, "Will you give me a second to explain Grayson? I swear, you're so damn impatient. It is a bit irritating to be honest."

I hit Grayson. "I only met you today and I completely agree with your brother."

Cayne smiled at me. "Oh, brother, I *really* like this one." Cayne continued, "As I was saying, I have heard about this before." He pointed at his book. "Ah, here we go!" He read out loud, "…a fire sensation between two Fae…"

He started to read silently as Grayson screamed out, "Cayne! For God's sake, give me the book." Cayne handed over the book, dumbfounded. Grayson looked at me and then finished reading from it, out loud, "...It is said that the original Faes who started the Fae war were once lovers. Their love was stronger than any other and when the Light Fae's father found out he was in love with a Dark Fae female, he had them cursed by a spiritual Fae."

Grayson looked at me. "The sparks that were once from a passionate love turned into a destructive fire that poisoned them into hating each other. Any other Faes who have experienced this sensation have suffered the same fate."

Chapter Five

Grayson threw the book on the table, "That is bullshit! How does whoever wrote this know what's happened to *every* Fae who has experienced this?" I stayed quiet, still in shock.

Cayne cleared his throat, "Um, Grayson. Calm down brother. You may be right, but I couldn't find anything else in our libraries."

Grayson interrupted, "We will all have to keep looking. I mean, we really don't have anything to freak out about, Aria hasn't even been through her Reckoning." They both looked at me, waiting for me to speak.

I cleared my throat, "Um, I mean you're kind of right. I haven't even started preparing for it."

They looked at each other and Cayne spoke up. "Aria, have you ever considered life as a Dark?"

Is he kidding me right now? Me? A Dark Fae? Hell to the no.

I stayed quiet for a few minutes and then finally answered him, "To be honest, the thought has never crossed my mind. Not even once. I am fairly certain I'll be staying Light. My entire family is Light."

Grayson added on, "Are you sure your *entire* family is Light?"

I stood up in protest, "Grayson, yes. I am sure. I'm ready to go home now. Can you please get me there before my parents have one of their tracker buddies out here?"

Cayne stood. "She's right, Grayson. It is getting late and you two have school tomorrow. Why don't you all head out of here and I'll do a little more digging?"

Grayson nodded, shook his brother's hand and smiled at me, "After you, madam." I hid my annoyance with a smile as we walked back to his fancy BMW.

The car ride home was fairly quiet and when we finally made it to my house, Grayson sighed, "Aria, don't be upset with me. I was just asking if you were sure your entire family has chosen to stay Light. There was no ill intent behind the question."

I unbuckled my seatbelt with a little more energy than necessary and looked at him. "Grayson, I'm not talking about this tonight. I do not want to think about my Reckoning before I have to."

Grayson let his eyes Light up a bright violet. "Aria, being Dark doesn't always translate into being bad. There's so much for you to know. Just promise me you'll at least educate yourself before making a decision?"

I opened my door and mumbled, "Bye, Grayson."

As I walked inside, Declan was running down the stairs. "Mom, Dad, Aria's finally home from her date!"

I threw my bracelet at him. "Shut up, loser. You don't have to announce it to the world."

He laughed as my parents walked into the foyer from the kitchen. My mom smiled at me. "I'm glad you're home on time."

My dad interjected, *"On time?* I'm glad you're home early. Everything go okay tonight?"

I looked at them both and gave them the worst fake-smile possible. "Ye-yeah, I'm fine. It's just been such a long day I needed to get home and get some rest."

My dad looked like he didn't really believe me, but didn't push on for anything more than I offered. "Alright, why don't you all call it a night? You two have school tomorrow and then we're going to go over the scripture you'll need to start practicing, Aria."

Declan and I looked at each other, rolled our eyes and in unison replied, "Goodnight."

The next morning, my breakfast routine was pretty normal. I couldn't get Grayson or the conversation we had last night out of my mind. *What if Dark Fae aren't all bad? Could I go Dark? Would I be happy as a Dark Fae? Aria, shut up, you're not thinking clearly. Go to school, blend in with the mundanes and tell Grayson you two cannot hang out again.* Alexia's strong push snapped me out of my day dream. "Dude, are you alright?".

I smiled. "Uh, yeah. Why do you ask?"

She glared at me, up and down. "Um, because I asked if you needed a ride and you totally ignored me. Don't be so rude, Aria."

My mom looked at us. "You two settle down. You all should be leaving before you're late."

As I told Alexia I would need a ride after school, Grayson's BMW pulled up next to us in the school parking lot. He rolled down his windows and smiled at me. Alexia lowered her sunglasses and looked at me, and then him, "Aria, *who is that?* Are you going to introduce me?"

I closed her door as I yelled out. "Bye, Alexia!"

I turned around, glared at Grayson and then started to walk towards Shantel. She was waving at me, with excitement in her eyes, "Hey girl! Hurry up!" I rolled my eyes and sped up my walk. *What is she so excited about this morning?*

Exhausted, I smiled at my best friend, "Hey Shantel, what's up?"

She signaled me to lean in for a secret. "There's a totally, hot new guy in Mr. Sulks' class. I mean, he's like *level ten hot.*"

I stepped back from her. "Seriously Shawns? Our second day at school and you've got a crush on a 'hot new' guy?"

She laughed. "Um, yeah. It is our second day but don't *you* have a major crush on the *other* new guy? And didn't you two meet *yesterday? On our first day of school?*"

"What ev. I don't have a crush on him, but who's this new guy you're talking about?"

She looked around. "Hm, he was just here, *weird.* He must have walked to class already." I started walking towards the school's entrance when Shantel asked, "Are we not going to wait for your new boyfriend? That's a bit rude, Aria."

I laughed. "He's definitely not my boyfriend." *I wish he was, but sadly, he can't ever be. We can't ever be.*

We walked into the building as Shantel continued to show her excitement for life. "Dude, aren't you so excited it's Friday? I mean I cannot wait to go to the beach tomorrow. It's supposed to be super pretty out.

We're going to the beach tomorrow, right?" I nodded and we walked into Mr. Sulk's class.

We took our seats as Grayson walked in and sat next to me. "Hey Aria, how are you today?" Shantel looked back at us with her smile showing from ear to ear.

I looked at him. "Hey. I'm okay, thanks." A few seconds later Mr. Sulks started his daily lesson and as I was taking notes, I noticed there was a crumpled piece of paper next to my foot.

I rolled my eyes, looked at Grayson, and then opened the note. "Hey, I'm sorry about last night. Don't be mad at me. I promise, no more Reckoning talk, okay?"

I looked at him, *God he's so perfect.* His hair had that sexy bedhead style. I replied, "Okay." *Aria, seriously? What happened to not talking to him anymore? It's okay. We can be friends, right*? I let a couple of minutes pass until I looked at him and when I did, I thanked the heavens I was sitting down. He was smiling at me with his perfect smile.

A second later, I nearly jumped out of my seat when the classroom door opened. It was Principal Lefton. He cleared his throat. "Excuse me, Mr. Sulks, I've got a new student I'd like to introduce you all to."

Mr. Sulks set down the tablet he was working on. "No problem, bring him or her in to my kingdom."

Mr. Lefton turned his attention to us. "Students, I want you all to welcome Ethan Whitelace."

Chapter Six

Wait, did he just say Ethan—Whitelace? That's—im—impossible. Shantel glanced back at me, with her eyes mirroring my own confusion. I looked over at Grayson who was frowning and looking down at his phone. He whispered to me, "Are you two related?"

It took everything inside of me to sit still and keep my composure. I leaned over and tried to reply as quiet and calmly as possible. "I have no idea. I mean, I've never really met a Whitelace I didn't know."

Mr. Sulks interrupted our conversation with his introduction of Ethan. "Class, this is Ethan. Ethan Whitelace, this is the class. You can take a seat," Mr. Sulks scanned the classroom for an open seat, "Hmm you can take a seat in front of Grayson."

I looked over at Grayson and the smile that sent my heart into a frenzy that morning was long gone. He returned my look with a raised eyebrow as Ethan approached us. Ethan took the seat in front of Grayson, but not before he turned around, faced me and gave a smirk that made every hair on my body stand up on its end. He turned back around and started taking notes from Mr. Sulks' lecture. The second class let out, I sprinted towards the hallway. I needed to call my mom.

Grayson was quickly by my side, trying to catch his breath. "Aria, wait up. We have got to talk!"

I nodded in agreement as I pulled out my cellphone. "Yeah, we definitely do. I have to get a hold of my mom first. Her family are the Whitelaces. She'd know if we were related."

Grayson cleared his throat, "Um, I don't know if you picked up on the guy's energy, but he's a Dark Fae. My parents may have him logged in their offices. They are the Royals after all."

That's right. If we were related and he was a Dark Fae, Grayson's family would have to know. I shook my head. "Why don't you call your parents and I'll call mine?"

He stopped me. "Aria, no. I can't go to my parents with any of this until I know he is in fact a relative of yours."

I slowed down my breathing. "Okay, I'm going to talk to my parents right after school and then I'll call you and let you know."

Grayson walked me to my next class and as we met up with Shantel, we saw *him*. Ethan was standing right in front of my locker.

Shantel whispered, "Aria, are you two related? He totally gives me the creeps." I shook my head and we all started walking closer to him. As we approached him, he waved at me. I looked at Grayson, and then Shantel and told her I'd catch up with her later.

When Grayson and I were standing in front of Ethan, he cleared his throat and winked at me with his bright, violet eyes. "Hey there, cuz. I know it's been a long time, but there's no need to be so rude."

Chapter Seven

I looked at Grayson and then at Ethan. "What the hell do you mean, '*cuz*'? We're *not* related."

Ethan let out a devilish laugh. "Oh, you have so much to learn. We are in fact family." He stepped closer to me, "And get this, not only am I your cousin, but I'm your Dark Fae cousin."

I pushed him away as Grayson stepped in between us. He mumbled to Ethan. "How are you a Dark Fae, in this school? Have you reported this to our council? Do my parents know you're here?"

Ethan laughed and rubbed his shoulder. "Cuz, don't get so aggressive towards me." He turned to Grayson, "My mother is actually meeting with your little council as we speak.

And why does it matter if your parents know that I'm here?"

Grayson let out a Dark laugh. "You're such an idiot. My parents are the Dark Royals, I'd watch the way you talk to me."

Ethan tilted his head, "Well, well, well. This is *so* interesting. So, 'Mr. Royal', does your family know you're in a relationship with a Light? I don't think that your mommy will be so welcoming to *that* cousin of mine." He looked at me. "No offense, cuz. It's not your fault that your parents chose the wrong side. From what I understand, you still can make a choice, am I right?"

"To be honest, that's none of your business..."

Before I could finish, Ethan cut me off. "...Look, cuz, I didn't come here to start trouble. I just moved here with my mom, you know, *your aunt.* Believe it or not, not all Dark Fae are evil. I mean, you're dating one, so you should be able to understand that. Right?"

I looked at Grayson as he answered for me. "If you're not here for trouble, you won't mention seeing Aria and I together then, right?"

Ethan laughed. "Whatever you say, master. On a serious note, I just want to be able to fly under the radar here. Do you think you all could show me around?"

*Does he actually think I'm going to be his friend? I can't be his friend, right? I mean, he's right, I haven't chosen a side and he **is** my family.* I finally spoke up, "Yeah, I can show you around. Take this as you will, but the minute you try to cause some trouble around here, you'll regret it."

Grayson added, "I agree. If you cause an ounce of a problem, I will report you to my parents myself. I don't care what you *think* you'll have hanging over my head."

Ethan threw his hands up in surrender. "Okay guys, sheesh. We're all in high school, we don't have to be so serious. But I got it, no trouble." He looked at Grayson and I and smiled. "So, just for my own curiosity, are you two actually dating?"

I hit him. "Again, none of your business. And just so you know, if anyone asks, we are distant cousins—that's all, got it?"

He put his hands on my shoulders. "Cuz, Lighten up. I am a Dark Fae, I'm not Satan. If you learn a little about the Dark Fae you may actually like us a bit more." He looked at Grayson, "Am I right, my friend?"

Grayson rolled his eyes and walked off as his cellphone rang. I looked at Ethan up and down as he was looking around the school's hallway. I asked, "Ethan, I really didn't know about you, or your mom. How long has it been since she's spoken to my mom? Does my mom know that you two are here?"

Ethan smiled. "Aria, I honestly didn't expect you to know about us. I know that once a Light has gone Dark, their family acts as if they never existed. That's pretty sad if you ask me. Your mom and my mom haven't talked since my mom turned and I don't think your parents know we're here. At least not yet. My mom was going to stop by this evening."

I choked out, "Are you serious? Your mom is going to my house? Um, I don't know if that's such a good idea. We're starting my Reckoning rituals after school."

Ethan laughed. "Oh really? That's interesting. Well, yeah, you all might have a little company." Before he could go on, Grayson walked back up to us.

Grayson cleared his throat, "Aria, may I speak to you, alone?"

I looked at him, and then my cousin. "Ethan, do you mind if we catch up after school?"

Ethan shook his head. "Nah, I don't mind. That's cool. See you later, cuz." He looked at Grayson. "See you later, your Highness."

After Ethan walked into a classroom down the hall, Grayson pulled me closer to him. "Aria, I think you need to go home. I think you need to go home and talk to your parents, now."

I looked at him, confused. "Why? What's wrong? Who called you?"

He sighed. "It was Cayne. He said that Ethan's mom *did* go to our home to present herself to my family."

I hurried him. "Okay, and...?"

He let out another sigh, "Well, his mom is Violet Whiteface, and she is a natural."

She's a Dark, natural Fae? "Holy shit."

He went on. "Yeah, exactly. You know that a natural, Dark Fae that has turned from the Light is nothing but trouble. She's one of the strongest Fae in the city now. Hell, she's probably stronger than everyone except my parents. That could be an issue." He held my hand. "Aria, please, go home and tell your parents. I don't trust your aunt being here."

After a few minutes I ran out of the hallway and then out of the school. Grayson let me use his car to drive home and on the way home I kept trying to call Alexia. I kept getting her voicemail. "God dammit Alexia. It's Aria, I need you to meet me at home! Now!"

I pulled up to the house and saw a silver SUV parked in front of the house. *Holy shit. I hope that's not who I think it is.* I hurried inside and saw my mom standing beside my dad. They looked at me as I closed the door and I saw a woman sitting on our sofa.

My mom cleared her throat, with tears in her eyes, "Aria, this is my sister. Th-this is your aunt, Violet."

Chapter Eight

I walked into the living room. "What the hell are *you* doing here?" I looked at my mom and dad. "Why is she here? Why haven't you two ever told me about her?" My dad and mom took a seat next to me.

Violet's eyes lit up as she stared at me up and down. "That is no way to talk to your elders. I'm here because I'm your family."

My dad interrupted, "She *was* family." He looked at me, "Aria, we haven't told any of you about her because she's nothing but trouble. She's a painful memory your mother and I wanted to leave behind."

Violet cleared her throat. "There's no need for insults, Liam." She stood up. "I can see I'm clearly not welcome here, and I don't stay where I'm not wanted."

My mom spoke now. "That's not true. You're always happy to show up where you're not welcome."

Violet's eyes lit up with fury. "You all do not want to upset me. I did not come here with any malicious intent. I just wanted to stop by to say hello to my dearest nieces and nephew." She looked at me again but spoke to my parents. "From what I understand, Aria's Reckoning preparations are about to begin?"

My dad shouted, "That is none of your business, Violet!"

Violet laughed, "Actually, Liam, it is. Have you forgot the Fae laws?"

I looked at my parents as they stayed quiet. "What is she talking about? Why is it any of her business?"

My mom whispered, "Oh God."

Violet giggled. "Oh, sister. Your God has nothing to do with this."

My dad stood up. "Violet, it's time for you to leave. I want you out of our home, now!"

Violet walked towards the front door, looked back at me and winked. "I'll be seeing you soon, Aria."

The second the door closed, I leaped up from the sofa and looked at my parents. "Mom, Dad, what the hell is she talking about? What Fae laws is she referring to?"

My dad spoke first, as my mom was still crying. "Aria, can we discuss this later? Please?"

I shook my head and screamed out, "No! We can't talk about this later, I need to know now. I don't know if you all know or not, but Violet has a son." They just looked at me, but still said nothing. I went on, "She has a Dark Fae son who just enrolled at my school. His name is Ethan."

Before they could say anything, the front door opened. Alexia and Declan walked in, laughing. Alexia looked from my parents to me, and said, "Um, is everything okay here? What's going on?"

I looked at her. "Everything is not okay. Declan you should go upstairs."

He shouted back at me, "Don't tell me what to do, Aria. You're not my mom!"

My mom spoke up. "Declan, listen to your sister. You need to go upstairs. Alexia, please come here."

Declan stomped upstairs as Alexia sat next to me in the living room. She looked at me. "Aria, you're shaking. What's wrong?"

I looked at her and then at our parents. "Ask them. They'll tell you everything. They'll tell us, *everything*."

My dad cleared his throat as he was about to start talking, but my mom interrupted. She wiped the tears from her eyes, "Alexia, we haven't been honest with you all. Our family hasn't always chosen to stay in the Light community."

Alexia stayed quiet and I pushed on. "Tell her, mom, tell her that your sister, our aunt, came here. Tell her that you've been hiding relatives from us. Tell her that we have Dark Faes in our family!"

My dad shouted at me, "Aria, I know you're upset but you will not talk to your mother that way. You've got it?"

My sister spoke before I could say anything. "What the hell is Aria talking about? We have an aunt?"

My mom took my dad's hand in hers. "Yes, you do. My sister, Violet, was a Light Fae who chose to go Dark during her Reckoning. The second she chose we were ordered by our parents to cut all ties with her. She left our home and council to join the Dark."

Alexia looked at me and whispered. "Now I know why you're so pissed."

My mom went on, "Girls, you all know the laws. I was young when Violet chose to go Dark. My parents *demanded* she leave our home the second she showed her true powers."

I cut her off. "You all know that she's a natural, right?"

The room got silent for a few moments until my mom cried out to my dad, "Liam, you know why she's here!"

My dad stayed quiet, so I asked, "Mom, why is she here? What does she want?"

My dad was hugging my mom when he turned to look at me and my sister. "She's here to turn you Dark."

Chapter Nine

"Last night was hell at my house." I was talking with Grayson on the phone as my mom knocked on my door. I cleared my throat. "Pick me up in an hour, I gotta go." I hung up the phone as my mom walked into my room.

She was smiling at me as she took a seat on my chaise. "Aria, we need to talk about yesterday." I threw my phone on my nightstand and she went on, "I haven't told any of you about Violet because it was just too painful of a memory to share with any of you."

I interrupted, "Mom, you should never have hidden a relative from us. Why couldn't you just tell us that you had a sister who went Dark? We would've understood why we hadn't met her."

My mom sighed. "Sweetie, I don't think that you understand why I chose to hide her from you all."

I stood up. "You're right. I don't understand, why don't you just tell me? Quit beating around the bush already, Mom. Violet is here and Ethan is in my school now. There's no reason to keep pretending like they're not real anymore."

My mom stood up next to me. "Aria, your aunt Violet killed your grandparents." Tears started to run down my mother's face and she ran out of the room.

After I was able to digest what my mom told me about my aunt, I called Grayson to pick me up. We went to our secret *place* and I started to tell him and his brother about what my mom revealed to me this morning.

The second I told them, Grayson erupted. "What the hell? are you serious? Aria, you're kidding, right?"

I shook my head. "I wish I was. My mom said that my aunt Violet killed my grandparents and absorbed their powers when she did it. That's how she became a natural."

We all stayed quiet for a second. I finally asked Cayne, "How exactly does a Fae become a natural? I've only heard of a few of them. I thought that a natural Fae was born that way."

Cayne nodded. "Yeah, it's not a very *normal* occurrence. You're right, a natural is usually born into its powers. They're able to control and manipulate all of the earth's natural elements. Though, I haven't heard of one Fae absorbing another Fae's powers."

He started flipping through the pages of a book and after a couple of seconds he squealed out, "Aha! Here we go…" He stayed quiet for a few seconds and I looked over at Grayson who was pacing in circles.

Grayson threw a book that he was holding across the room. "For God's sake, Cayne! Why do you do that? You can *not* keep saying, 'aha' and then read in silence! This isn't a damn TV show, we don't need the dramatics. What did you find?"

Cayne looked up. "Calm down, brother." He looked at me. "Are you sure you want to date someone with his temper?" He cleared his throat and went on, "Okay, well there have only been two recorded instances where a Fae has absorbed another's powers." He set the book down. "I'm not sure you all really want to know what this says."

Grayson rolled his eyes. "I'm feeling *really* confident with how well you know me, brother."

Cayne laughed. "Okay well, don't say I didn't warn you." Grayson sat down at the Dark oak table and his brother went on, "One of the Fae that wasn't born a natural absorbed and killed a stronger Fae of their original bloodline."

Grayson tapped his hands on the table. "We already know that's possible. How did the other Fae become a natural?"

Cayne looked up at us, and then continued to read from the book. "Well, the other Fae that did this is…" He got quiet, put the book down and sighed. "Crap…" He went on, "another Fae that did this was…Sebastian Harper."

After a couple of awkward seconds, Grayson sighed, "Holy shit. *You were right*, I didn't want to know that."

I looked at them, confused. I asked, "Who's Sebastian Harper?"

Cayne looked at me. "Aria, Sebastian is the *original* Dark Fae. He's the reason we're able to choose Dark or Light. He slaughtered his parents, siblings and children. His wife, Camila, is the original Light Fae. She is said to have been the strongest Fae around and represented all things good in life. She left her husband and instead of seeking revenge she pardoned him and forced him to live as a Dark for the remainder of his life."

I sighed. "*Wow*. So, Sebastian is the original Dark Fae who is *also* the original non-born natural?"

The guys looked at each other and then at me. Grayson nodded. "Yeah, Sebastian hasn't been seen in like, forever. My parents are Royals and they have never seen or heard from him."

I stood up. "Why is it that both the times we came here, we found out some pretty heavy stuff?"

Both the guys let out a stressed laugh. Grayson spoke after a couple of seconds. "Why do your parents think that Violet is here to turn you Dark?"

Cayne answered as I shrugged my shoulders, "It's because Aria is their second child. The second child of a family that has both Light and Dark Fae are required to learn both scriptures for their Reckoning." He looked at me. "If you didn't have a Dark Fae in your family, you would be able to begin your preparations like any other Fae. But because your aunt Violet is a Dark, you're required to spend time with a Dark Fae to learn their scriptures."

I sighed. "What if I don't want to learn about the Dark side? I can't choose Dark, my family is Light."

Grayson spoke now, "Aria, I've told you before, not all Dark Faes are bad. Some choose Dark because of the different powers we're able to do that Light Faes can't."

Cayne added, "I know the last time you were here you made it clear that you didn't want to talk about this, but with Violet here, I think it's better you learn from us. She killed your grandparents for her own selfish reasons. We haven't killed anyone. Give us the chance to teach you a bit."

I sat back down. "Let me talk about it with my parents. Until I talk to them about all of this I won't be learning anymore about the Dark scriptures."

Both the guys nodded as Cayne's cell phone rang. He immediately answered, "Hello? Are you kidding me? Where? Is Briar there? Okay, we're on our way."

Grayson stood up. "What's up? Who was that?"

Cayne looked at us. As he responded his face grew paler. "It was Natalia. Someone burned down the Light Fae council chambers. Briar is there and needs us to help out with the investigation."

Grayson looked confused. "If the Light's chambers were burnt down, why are we helping with the investigation?"

Cayne looked at me as he answered, "A Dark Fae is the suspect."

Chapter Ten

Grayson, Cayne and I were at the Light Faes' council chambers in a matter of minutes. When we started walking toward the burnt building, my heart stopped. I looked at Grayson. "I can't go in there. My parents are here."

He looked around and then asked, "Are you sure? I don't see their car here?" He stared at all the Fae around us. "I don't think they're here. You'll be fine, come on."

I shook my head. "No, they *are* here." I pointed at Alexia's car. "They're in Alexia's car, you see?"

The minute I finished my sentence, I heard my mom's voice. She called out, "Aria? What are you doing here?"

Crap. I slowly turned around. "Oh, hey Mom. I was working on a project with one of my classmates when I heard about the chambers being burnt down. I asked him to bring me."

Alexia walked up. "Hey sis, things are insane right now. Have you heard? Lucas is missing."

"Who's Lucas?"

"Aria, he's our council leader. No one knows where he's at. He's not picking up his cell phone and the council members are losing their mind."

I gasped. "What do you mean he's missing? How'd he go missing?" I turned to my mom. "Didn't he have the guard there to protect him?"

My mom sighed. "I don't know anything yet Aria. It's being investigated now. We've had to call some Dark Faes to investigate. I've heard a Dark Fae is the suspect."

I looked at her and then at my dad as he walked up. "You all don't think it was her, do you? There's no way Violet would do this, right?"

My dad put his hand on my shoulder. "We're really not sure. We're waiting for the Dark Fae to send some council members to do their part of the investigation. You know that every Fae has a unique imprint. We're hoping they can use that to track down whoever is responsible for this."

Alexia looked at me. "Sis, you didn't bring a mundane here, did you?"

I looked around. "Oh, um. No, I came with Grayson. He's in my history class and we had a project we had to work on."

My family members looked at me, confused. My dad spoke, "If you didn't bring a mundane, but came with a boy, who is he? Where is he?"

I looked towards Grayson and Cayne's direction. They were both talking to a guy who had Light brown hair and stood just as tall as Cayne. I assumed it was their brother, Briar.

My sister followed my eyes and then gasped, "Aria, you're dating a Treble? You know they're *the Royals*, right?"

My parents both stayed quiet and stared at Grayson. After a second my mom screamed out, "Aria Whitelace, you will not date a Treble! You know that is against our laws!"

My dad added, "Aria, I am so disappointed in you. You haven't been through your Reckoning but you know that dating or talking to a Dark Fae is unacceptable. You will not speak to him again. You got it?"

No, I don't 'got it'. There's no way in hell anyone is going to tell me who I can or cannot date. I screamed out, "You all cannot tell me who I can talk to!" I stared into my dad's eyes. "You're right. I haven't gone through my Reckoning so technically, I can, and will, talk to whoever the hell I want!"

My mom started crying. "Aria, this is what *she* wanted. Violet wants you to turn against us. You don't think for a second that the Treble boy doesn't know who did this? Aria, he's one of them."

Alexia just stared at me, without speaking. Tears were starting to run down my face when I responded to my mom. "All of you are right. He *is* a Treble. He *is* a Dark Royal. And he's *going to* be my boyfriend."

Chapter Eleven

Before I could finish the conversation with my family, Grayson was standing by my side. He extended his hand to my dad. "Mr. Whitelace, I'm Grayson Treble, it's a pleasure to meet you."

My dad looked at me and then at him, grabbing my mom's hand. "I wish I could say the same. What are you doing with my daughter? You have gone through your Reckoning. You know that this *thing* you all have is forbidden."

Grayson put his hand down and made a grunting sound, "With all due respect, what I'm doing with your daughter has *nothing* to do with you. You're right, I have gone through my Reckoning and I can and *will* talk to whoever I please. My parents are the Royals and, as you know, Aria has not gone through her Reckoning." He looked at me and went on, "With that being said, my parents approve of our relationship." He gave me his notorious grin and took my hand. "I wanted to ask you this later, but will you join my family and I for dinner tomorrow?"

My parents shouted out in unison, "She will not!"

My dad's face was filled with rage. "Aria will not be joining your family for anything. Especially since your *kind* are the reason our council's chambers have burnt down!"

Grayson stared at my dad; his eyes were glowing violet now. "I'm aware that this was the work of a Dark Fae. That is the reason my brothers and I are here. But if you want to go pointing fingers, you do realize it was probably *your* relative who was responsible for this, right?"

My mom spoke up. "She is not my relative! She was at one time, but this *thing* she's turned into is not my sister."

Briar and Cayne walked towards us. Cayne asked, "Is everything okay, brother?" The twins' eyes were glowing violet as they stood next to Grayson.

I turned my attention to my parents and noticed that their eyes were now glowing with a mixture of blue and gray. I spoke, hoping to break the tension. "Hey guys, everything is okay. Did you all find anything?"

Cayne kept his focus on my parents while he answered me. "We could not figure out the imprint of the Fae who did this. If it were a high skilled natural, she would have the knowledge to alter her imprint."

I asked, "Are you saying it was Violet who did this?"

Briar answered now. "It looks like it was *definitely* your aunt. We don't have another natural who is registered with our family in town. We've notified our parents' guards. They're on the way to her home to question her."

Cayne added, "I know some Fae may believe that the Dark are nothing but 'bad guys', but we don't go burning buildings down for fun."

72

My dad stood in front of my mom, eyes fully blue now. "If you all found what you came for, may I suggest you leave?"

The Treble brothers stayed quiet for a few awkward seconds, when Grayson finally spoke up. "Aria, we better go. Go home with your parents, text me later and let me know about dinner tomorrow?"

I nodded my head as he leaned in to kiss me. Alexia let out a shriek as my parents both pulled me away from him.

Grayson let his eyes glow brighter as he smiled at them. "It was a pleasure meeting you all."

We sat in silence the whole way home. I could feel the anger radiating off of my family. Alexia, usually a free spirit, would not even look at me. My dad parked the car in our driveway and got out of the vehicle without saying a word to me.

When my dad walked inside of our home, my mom looked back at me. "Aria, I hope you think about what you're putting us through. Our council's chambers have been burnt down,

Lucas is missing and now we have to deal with *this*."

I barked back at her, "You have to deal with *this*? You mean you have to deal with me?"

My mom tried to keep her composure, her eyes Lighting up a tint of blue again. "Aria, go to bed and think about what you're doing. We're starting your Reckoning preparations in the morning. You won't be going to school and you sure as hell will not be going to dinner with that boy."

I got out of our vehicle, slammed the door and stomped indoors.

When I got into my room I called Grayson. He immediately answered. "Aria? Is everything okay?"

With tears running down my face, I asked, "Are you and your brothers still willing to teach me about the Dark Faes' history?"

Chapter Twelve

Grayson stayed quiet for a minute and then answered me. "Aria, you've got to be kidding, right?"

I huffed. "No, Grayson. I'm not kidding. I'm sick of everyone telling me what to do and when to do it. I am only just going to start my Reckoning preparations tomorrow and I've already got my parents breathing down my throat."

He cleared his throat. "I don't want you to feel like I'm forcing you to do anything. You have plenty of time before you go through your Reckoning so we'll be fine, for now."

Tears started to run down my face. "Will you please just come over tomorrow and help me with my first day of Reckoning preparation?"

He released a nervous sigh. "Aria, I don't know if that's a good idea. Especially after what happened tonight. I need to talk to my parents about it and then I'll let you know, okay?"

I tried to hold back my sobs. "O-okay. I really need you here tomorrow. If not, I'm afraid Violet's going to be the one who teaches me the Dark's scriptures."

Grayson grunted. "Yeah, *that's* not going to happen. I'll see you in the morning."

My alarm went off the next morning and as I crawled out of my bed, I noticed my cell phone was flashing with notifications. Grayson sent me a text message, "I can't wait to see you. Be there in a while. – Grasyon".

Crap. I have to tell my parents Grayson is coming over. I screamed out, "Mom, Dad, can you come up here please?"

A few seconds later, my parents were both knocking on my door. My mom took a seat next to me on my bed. My dad asked, "Aria, what's going on?"

I started to nervously toss my stuffed animal, Mr. Tobbly, around. "Um, I'm sorry about last night. I shouldn't have talked to you all the way I did."

My mom put her hand on my shoulder. "I know it's a lot to take in. And I know that you are experiencing a lot of different feelings right now. I'm sorry for snapping at you the way I did, too."

My dad took a seat next to my mother and me. "Aria, last night was a bad night for all of us. Your mother and I talked and we think it'd be okay for you to learn the Dark scriptures from Grayson."

My mom added, "We're not okay with it, but it is better than you having to spend time with Violet."

I nodded. "I agree. And I'm glad you all feel that way. I called you all up here because Grayson agreed to teach me the scriptures. He said he'd be here this morning."

My parents looked at each other and then my dad spoke up. "Honey, it's going to take us a while to get used to this. I hope you know that."

My mom grabbed my dad's hand. "We're going to really try to be understanding, but you know that the decision will have to be yours. You will need to listen to your heart."

My dad finished, "You can't decide Light or Dark, for us or for him. Your mom is right. Your heart will tell you what to do."

I started crying. "Why do I have to decide? Why can't I just be me and be happy?"

My mom rubbed my shoulders as my dad kissed the top of my head. My mom spoke first. "Baby, I know it seems like a tough decision, but it's something our kind has done for centuries. It's just the way our lives are."

My dad continued my mom's thought. "Once you've learned both the Light and Dark scriptures, you'll know what you want. Grayson may be a kind young man. He won't be the last you meet, though."

I wiped the tears from my eyes. "He is great. I don't know that I'll ever feel this way again."

My mom let out a nervous laugh. "Aria, I promise you, you most definitely will."

I shook my head. "No, I don't think I will. Mom, Dad, when we first touched, we felt a spark. It wasn't a metaphoric spark. We actually both felt a fire in our touch."

My parents gasped at the same time just as Alexia and Declan came into my room. Declan spoke, "Hey you guys, there's a boy waiting for Aria downstairs."

Chapter Thirteen

As we went downstairs to meet Grayson, my parents were murmuring to each other. I heard my dad say, "Adalyn, we have to take this to the council. If what Aria is saying is true, there's a good chance…"

My mom cut him off. "…Don't say it, Liam. Let's just get this day over with and then we'll talk to the council about it."

I got to the foot of the steps and saw *him* staring up at me. His eyes were glowing violet. He smiled. "Aria, you look lovely this morning."

My dad grunted. "Grayson, welcome to our home. I am sorry about the way we ended things last night."

My mom added, "I'm thankful you agreed to teach Aria your scriptures. My husband and I talked things over and we both agree that it's better she learn them from you than from her aunt."

Grayson nodded. "I agree. And Mr. Whitelace, I completely understand that you're just trying to protect your daughter." He winked at me. "She's an amazing young lady and I just want to give her the opportunity to learn both sides. When the time comes, she can make her own decision."

My dad let off a half-smile while gesturing for us to sit in the living area. My parents sat next to each other and Grayson took the seat next to me. My dad put his hand on my mom's. "Grayson, you say your family is okay with the *relationship* that you and Aria have. Are they okay with you sharing your knowledge of Dark Fae with Aria?"

Grayson looked at me and then turned his attention to my parents. "Yes sir, they are fine with it. And speaking of my parents, they would like for you all to come to our home for dinner."

My mom shifted uncomfortably and before either of my parents could respond, Grayson continued, "We know that the Dark and Light are not supposed to interact with one another, but my parents are very *progressive*. They believe we see the world different from one another, but that doesn't make one better than the other."

My dad lifted his hand from my mom's and spoke up. "Grayson, I appreciate your parents' invitation, I just don't know if that is something that our council would agree with. We would have to get clearance from them. Especially since our chambers were just burnt to a crisp because of a Dark Fae."

Grayson pushed on. "I'm sure your council will agree to it once you tell them that our council has found the Fae accused of this crime."

My parents gasped. My mom asked, "You have? Was it...my sister?"

Grayson took a deep breath. "Yes, it was. She had help covering her imprint though."

My mom went on, "Are you sure? She's a natural. She would have the capability to do that, you know."

Grayson nodded. "Yes ma'am. We are aware she's a natural but there's evidence that another, stronger Fae was also involved."

My mom pushed Grayson for more information. "What do you mean, another Fae was involved?"

Grayson looked around, nervously. "Um, I think that you should really talk with my parents. That is another reason they want to meet with you."

My dad spoke before my mom could. "Grayson, let us get the okay from our council and we will be there. I get the sense that something bad is going on and I appreciate your family wanting to keep us informed."

Grayson sighed in relief. "Yes sir. I don't know all of the details but I imagine something is happening that they need to let your council know about."

My parents nodded as I changed the subject and asked, "Are we going to start my training today?"

My mom smiled at me. "Yes, we are. Let's get started with the Light and Dark scriptures."

Chapter Fourteen

The following days flew by. Grayson came over every day to teach me the Dark scriptures. My parents still weren't too fond of him, but they got the okay from our council to attend a dinner with the Trebles.

Grayson interrupted my thoughts. Crap, I forgot he was on speaker phone. He groaned. "Aria, I'm on my way home now. What time will you and your parents be there?"

I looked at my reflection in the mirror and thought about changing my outfit when I heard Grayson mumble something about me ignoring him.

I laughed. "Sorry, yeah, we will be there in about half an hour. See you soon."

He cleared his throat. "Sounds good. See you soon, hot stuff."

As I ended our call, an unknown number texted me. "Hey cuz, meet me at the school around midnight. We've got to talk."

I scratched my head as I responded. "Is this Ethan? Are you insane?"

As I finished getting ready, he responded. "Yeah, it's me. I'm not insane but you don't want to upset me. Meet me there and come alone."

I rolled my eyes. "K."

What the hell does he want to meet me for? I'm sure he's heard about what his mom did. I wonder if he knows what she's got planned.

My mom interrupted my thoughts as she yelled out, "Aria, we're heading to the car. Come on down, we can't be late to the Trebles."

We drove for about twenty minutes before the GPS notified us we had reached our destination.

I asked, "Did you all know this was a gated community?"

My parents shook their heads. My dad answered me, "I don't think it's a community. This is their home."

My mouth fell open. As we were let in, I saw a mansion in the far distance. My mom spoke, "Do you think they need all this land? Is that size of a home necessary?"

My dad smiled. "Adalyn, don't be so judgmental. You forget, they are the Dark Royals. This is kind of like their palace."

I mumbled, "Their palace? Wow. This is going to be awkward."

We pulled in front of their home and were greeted by four men in black suits. My mom and dad looked a little annoyed as two of the men held open our doors and asked for the keys so they could park the car for us.

My mom looked at my dad. "Valet, seriously Liam?"

He laughed as he held her hand. "Let's make the best of this night, okay?"

Grayson stood at the front door, smiling with his violet eyes shining bright. He greeted us. "Hello Mr. and Mrs. Whitelace, Aria. Welcome to our home. Thank you for coming. I hope you all found it okay."

My dad extended his hand to Grayson. "Hello Grayson. Yes, we did. You all have got a lovely property. Are your parents inside?"

Grayson nodded. "Yes, they are. They're actually waiting for us inside."

I reached out for Grayson's hand as my parents trailed a few steps behind us. "Ethan texted me earlier."

Grayson's jawline tightened. "Oh yeah? What did he want?"

I shrugged my shoulders. "He wants me to meet him at school tonight."

He squeezed my hand and gestured for my mom and dad to enter the room ahead of us.

My mom smiled at the both of us as we heard a lady from inside the room speak. "Mr. and Mrs. Whitelace, it's my pleasure to meet you. My husband will be joining us shortly."

Grayson whispered, "We'll talk about your cousin in a bit."

He smiled at my parents. "Mr. and Mrs. Whitelace, this is my mother, Cherise. Mom, this is Mr. and Mrs. Whitelace."

Cherise stood shy of five feet with long, blonde hair. Her eyes were a beautiful, glowing violet. She smiled at my parents. "It's a pleasure to meet you both."

She glanced over their shoulders and looked at me. "And you must be Aria. I've heard so much about you. Thank you for keeping my Grayson out of trouble at that mundane school."

I laughed. "Nice to meet you too, Mrs. Treble."

My mom spoke, "Cherise, your home is lovely. Thank you for inviting us for dinner."

Before Mrs. Treble could respond, a tall, tanned man walked into the room. He looked at all of us and walked over to Cherise. He raised her hand, kissed her palm and then greeted my parents. "Welcome to our home, I'm Braden Treble. I'm so sorry I was running late. I had to handle a business call."

He walked closer to me and I felt like I was frozen in place. He gave me a smile that uncomfortably similar to Grayson's. "Aria, it is very nice to meet you. Grayson speaks very highly of you. From what I understand, you've already got the Dark scriptures down?"

I felt the blood in my face warm up. My dad cleared his throat. "Mr. Treble, your son has been quite the gentleman. Thank you for allowing him to help us with this situation."

Braden and Cherise looked at each other. Mr. Treble replied, "To be honest Mr. Whitelace, Grayson didn't get my vote of approval on the matter. My wife was the one who insisted. And you know the saying, 'happy wife, happy life'."

Cherise spoke now. "Shall we go into the dining hall before we begin this conversation?"

Chapter Fifteen

We walked into dining room where a line of Dark Fae stood and bowed as the Trebles walked past them. My mom and dad were a few steps ahead of Grayson and I. Grayson grabbed and squeezed my hand. I looked into his glowing eyes. He muttered, "Everything is going to be fine, right?"

I sure as hell hope so. I smiled at him. "Yeah, for sure."

My dad turned around and looked at us as Mr. Treble spoke. "Please, why don't you all sit here." He held out the chair for my mom as one of his guards held my dad's seat.

My mom was smiling from ear to ear. "Thank you, Mr. Treble."

Cherise signaled for Grayson to join her on the other side of the long, wooden dining table. He kissed my hand as I took the chair next to my dad.

As Grayson walked across the dining room my dad asked, "Will your other children be joining us this evening?"

Mr. and Mrs. Treble smiled at each other as Braden answered, "Unfortunately, they're all unavailable tonight. They all had prior engagements and we thought it'd be a bit more productive if it were just the six of us."

My dad responded, "Very well then, shall we address the elephant in the room, head on?"

Mr. Treble looked at his wife and then turned his attention back to us. "I like the kind of man you are, Liam."

My dad's jaw tightened as his eyes started to Light up with a blue-gray tint.

Mrs. Treble spoke, "Alright, well you both know that we sent some members of our council to investigate the crime that took place at your council's chambers."

My parents nodded in unison. Cherise went on, "We tried to pinpoint the Fae who was responsible for this crime by using trackers to look for their imprint. After a few failed attempts, one of our trackers was finally able to uncover not one, but two imprints."

My mom pushed on. "Who were these Fae? Were they not Dark?"

Mr. Treble responded, "One of the Fae involved was Violet Whitelace, your sister. And as you know, she is a Dark Fae."

My dad said, "She was my wife's sister. Who was the other Fae?"

Mr. Treble shifted in his chair uncomfortably. "We're actually still going over that imprint. Their imprint was not able to be fully recovered."

My dad protested. "What do you mean the imprint was unable to be recovered?"

Cherise answered, "Violet manipulated the other imprint with her own and had we not gone over the scene numerous times, I'm afraid we would have missed it altogether."

My mom's eyes were now glowing blue. "Will you be punishing Violet for this horrendous crime?"

Braden cleared his throat. "It's actually not that easy."

My mom cried out, "What do you mean, it's not that easy? You know she was at the scene of the crime. You know she purposely manipulated the other Fae's imprint. That alone is a crime!"

Cherise's eyes were glowing bright with anger as Grayson spoke. "What my parents aren't saying is that the other imprint cannot be 100% accurate because it is registering as Sebastian Harper."

Chapter Sixteen

My parents shouted out together, "Sebastian Harper? That's impossible!"

Mrs. Treble looked like she was trying to compose herself once again. "We agree and that is why we are still processing the data and have some of our best on the scene."

Mr. Treble added, "We were going to send some of our guards to detain Violet but we decided to wait until we could gather more evidence. If, for some strange reason, the imprint is Sebastian's, we'll need to make our next move appropriately."

Confused, I asked, "Isn't Sebastian the original Dark Fae? I thought he was long gone."

Grayson answered me, "We thought he was, too. If he isn't though, we are all in trouble. My family and yours, Light and Dark. If he is back, he has the ability to take control of our guard and cause chaos."

My dad demanded, "We must inform our council of this. Sebastian Harper being a possible suspect is something we should all prepare for. Do you all have any leads as to why or where Lucas was taken?"

Braden whispered, "We're afraid Lucas may be deceased. His imprint was on the scene, however it was very faint. Signs of a violent struggle were shown. Our council is working with yours as we speak. We've given our council our permission to work with them to get this resolved as soon as possible."

Cherise added, "I hope you all now know that even though we are Dark, we do not condone these kinds of acts."

She turned her attention to me. "Aria, I understand that Grayson has been helping you with your studies?" I nodded as she continued. "He also tells me that he has explained that Dark and Light Fae have different capabilities. I hope you know that is one of the only differences we have. Our being Dark has nothing to do with the type of Fae we are. We love one another just as your family does."

My mom warned, "Please, tread Lightly Mrs. Treble."

Cherise nodded. "I know that your family hasn't had the best impression of Dark Fae, but let me make myself clear. My family does not knowingly harm other Fae, or mundanes. We are a new kind of Dark Fae and believe that we can all with one another in peace."

Mr. Treble added, "My wife is correct. We're sorry that the Dark Fae you all have come across have not been the best, but we hope you allow us a chance to show you that Dark Fae can be good. Light and Dark does not translate into good and bad, at least not to us."

My dad asked, "How do you all know that the other Dark Fae think as you do?"

Braden responded, "We don't know that they do. However, how do you know that all Light Fae are in fact 'good'?"

Mrs. Treble continued her husband's thought. "All we are asking is that you all give our family a chance. Grayson has shown us that he is very fond of your daughter and we would like to put aside our differences for our children."

My mom asked, "What are you all suggesting? That we go against our council's ways and allow our daughter to hang around a Dark Royal?"

Grayson responded, "I think my parents are asking that you all speak to your council about their 'ways'. No offense Mr. and Mrs. Whitelace, but they're a bit outdated."

My dad's eyes were glowing a bright blue again. "No offense taken, Grayson. My wife and I are not on the council so all we do is follow their laws. We will take your concerns to them, but if they do not agree with your family's progressive thinking, I'm sorry."

Braden Treble let his frustration show. "There's no need for you to go to your council. We will arrange a meeting ourselves. We're speaking to you as parents, not as the Royal family. We cannot tell our children who they can and cannot date."

The tension in the room quickly rose. After a few awkward minutes, I decided to break the silence. "Um…I know my birthday is still a few months away, but I'm pretty sure I know what I'm going to choose."

Chapter Seventeen

I turned to my parents, who looked at me with worry in their eyes. My dad stood up. "I think it's best if we leave now. Mr. and Mrs. Treble, thank you for having us over tonight."

Before my mom could react, Cayne and Briar ran into the dining room. Cayne was yelling out, "Mom, Dad! You're not going to believe what we've..."

He stopped in his tracks as Briar spoke. "Oh, we're sorry." Briar looked at me. "Hello, Aria."

I smiled as Mrs. Treble stood up. "Hello boys, don't be rude to our guests."

The guys looked at each other and then bowed to my parents. "Hello, Mr and Mrs. Whitelace."

My dad cleared his throat. "Hello. We were just leaving."

Cayne shuffled some papers his hands. "With all due respect, I don't think you should leave right now. I think it's best you all hear what we've found this evening."

My dad hesitantly took his chair as Mr. Treble asked, "What is it, Cayne? What's going on?"

Cayne looked at Briar nervously. Briar answered his dad's question, "Well, we were looking into the imprint that was in question at the Light Fae's chambers. We have confirmation that the other imprint is indeed Sebastian Harper's."

The room got eerily quiet. I asked, "How is that possible? What does this all mean?"

Grayson looked at me. "I'm afraid Violet and Sebastian are working together. That can't be a good thing for any of us."

His mom added, "I'm afraid Sebastian is trying to reclaim his authority over the Dark

Fae. If this is true, not only are we in trouble, but all Fae will be in danger from this alliance."

My mom questioned, "How do you know that Sebastian is trying to claim his throne again? What does my sister have to do with this?"

Braden said, "Sebastian Harper does not believe in councils. He does not believe in any kind of democracy or progressive thinking. As for your sister, I'm not exactly sure why she'd be working for him. The two of them combined though, that's a deadly combination."

Cayne spoke up, "I think I know what Violet is doing…"

We all turned to him as his face paled. "I think that she is hoping to be his bride, or at the very least his partner in crime."

As soon as Cayne finished speaking, chaos erupted. Everyone started to demand answers as Mr. Treble shouted, "Silence, please! If Violet wants to align herself with Sebastian, I'm afraid our problems have only just begun."

He turned to face my parents. "Mr. and Mrs. Whitelace, I believe this is good time for us to end the evening. I think we should get in contact with your council."

My parents stood and nodded in agreement. My mom spoke, "You're probably right and I'm sorry we weren't able to enjoy an actual dinner. Hopefully the next time we meet it will be a bit less tense."

I don't want to leave. I want to be here, with him. I spoke, "Mom, Dad, what if Grayson took me home a little later? We have been putting off a school project because of all of this, I don't think our teacher would take our chambers being burnt down as an excuse."

My parents looked at me with reluctance. My dad finally answered me, "Aria, I'm not sure that is the best idea. I think it's best we go home so the Trebles can do what they need to. I would hate for you to be a burden."

Mrs. Treble smiled at me. "Aria will be no burden. Grayson can have her home before 11pm, if that's okay? She's right, they shouldn't neglect their school work."

My dad looked at my mom for confirmation and she returned Mrs. Treble's smile. "Alright then, Aria, no later than 11pm. You got it, missy?"

I hugged my mom and dad as they said their goodbyes to the Trebles.

We walked my parents to their car and when we got back inside Grayson put his arms around me. "Aria, can you believe that just happened? Our families agreeing to let us spend time together?"

I squeezed him closer to me. "Yeah, I think that the whole Violet and Sebastian thing is a little more serious than us hanging out."

He laughed and then stepped back. "Aren't you supposed to meet Ethan tonight?"

I sighed. "Crap, I forgot about that."

He called out for his brother, "Hey Cayne, can you come here please?"

Cayne walked towards us with a grin on his face. "What's up, lovebirds?"

Grayson's eyes lit up. "Ethan Whitelace texted Aria before she came over. He wants to meet up with her tonight, alone."

Cayne's grin disappeared. "Are you kidding? Why? What could he possibly want?"

I shrugged my shoulders. "I have no idea. He said that we needed to talk."

Cayne huffed as Grayson asked, "Do you think we should trail her to make sure everything is okay?"

Cayne answered his brother, "I don't think that's very smart. Ethan is a tracker. He'd be able to tell we were there, especially if he wants Aria to be alone. He'll be trying to sense any other Fae that may be close by."

Ethan's jaw tightened. "What do we do then? We can't let Aria go alone."

I spoke now. "He's my cousin. I don't think he'll try to hurt me. I feel like if he was going to set me up, he wouldn't want to meet me randomly at midnight."

Cayne looked at me with worry in his eyes. "Aria, I'm not sure about that. Violet is his mom. She did burn down your council's chambers. Don't you think his loyalty lies with her?"

I looked at the brothers as I answered Cayne. "I don't know where his loyalty lies. I don't know him. I guess there's only one way to find out though, right?"

Chapter Eighteen

Grayson was about to interject when Briar walked into the room. Briar looked at all of us and greeted me with a hug. "Aria, how was dinner with our parents? I'm sorry I couldn't make it. I had some council business to attend to."

I leaned into his hug. "Well, we didn't even get to the whole dinner part."

He took a step back from me and looked at his brothers. "Oh really? Everything okay? What happened?"

Cayne answered, "Yeah, everything's okay. I just filled them in with the whole Sebastian theory. As you could imagine, that kind of killed the vibe for the rest of our night."

Briar nodded as Grayson spoke up, "Aria's going to meet with Ethan, Violet's son. He asked her to meet with him, alone."

Briar's eyes lit up as he turned to me. "What does he want? Are you going? Can you trust him?"

I sighed. "I was just telling your brothers, I don't know what he wants and yes, I am going. I'm not sure if I can trust him but Cayne said that since Ethan's a tracker it's not smart if you guys go."

He looked at me with a tightened jaw. "I agree with my twin. We cannot follow you, undetected. If he's a skilled tracker, and I assume he is, it will be nearly impossible."

Grayson took my hand. "Aria, do what you feel is right."

I looked at him and put my lips on his hand. "I think I should go. I don't think he's going to set me up. I have a weird feeling about it. Not a bad feeling, but weird."

Cayne huffed. "Well, we will get as close to the school as we can, so if you need us we'll be just a phone call away."

Briar took my phone and entered his phone number as Cayne went on. "I'll tell Mom and

Dad we're heading out to the chambers while you two sneak out. Let's meet up at the corner store near the school."

We all nodded as Grayson walked me to the car.

Grayson dropped me off and with my nerves in my throat, I acted like I was preparing for bed as Alexia and Declan walked into my room.

Declan asked, "How was it at the Dark Royals'? Were their eyes lit up violet the entire time? Is it true that they can't control it?"

Alexia hit him as I answered his ridiculous questions. "Going to their house was just like going to any other person's house. No, their eyes weren't lit up the whole time and yes they can control it—sometimes."

Alexia pushed on, "So, what happened? Mom and Dad came in and were on their phones the entire evening. I'm surprised that they let you stay there without them. They must have liked the Trebles, huh?"

I shrugged. "Um, I don't know if they really liked them. Who were Mom and Dad talking to? What were they saying?"

Alexia looked at Declan. "Um, you should probably go to your room before Mom and Dad realize you're still awake."

Declan hit her and cried out. "You're not in charge of me anymore! Mom and Dad are here and if they wanted me asleep, they'd tell me!"

I walked over to him and hit him on the arm. "Fine, don't go to bed, but you need to get out of my room."

Alexia laughed as he ran out shouting. "Mom, Dad! Alexia and Aria are seriously working my nerves again!"

I looked over at my sister who rolled her eyes as she was looking at her cellphone. She put away the phone after a second and looked up at me. "Girl, spill the beans. I need to know what's going on."

I sat on the computer chair across from my bed. "Well, we did meet with the Royals. Did you know that they live in like, a mansion?"

Alexia's mouth dropped. "Shut up! That's insane. But wait, are you talking like a Beverly Hills mansion or the White House?"

I laughed. "A little of both. They had guys who opened the doors for us and Mom freaked because there was valet."

She started laughing with me. "I wish I was there to witness that."

I went on, "Anyways, everything was going okay until we were told that they found out what Fae Violet was working with."

My sister asked, "Well, who was it? Have they caught them? Are they going to strip their powers?"

I shook my head. "Not exactly. They actually found out that the other Fae was Sebastian Harper."

Alexia stood up. "Aria, quit lying. That's impossible. I thought he was dead."

I stood now. "I swear. When they said that, all hell broke loose. No one knows why he's back or why he's helping Violet."

She whispered, "So, what's going to happen?"

I shrugged. "I really don't know. All I know is that they're going to keep it from everyone. They won't be confronting Violet until they have a proper plan of action."

Alexia mumbled, "That's why Mom and Dad were on the phone all night. They're calling members of the council. Were the

Trebles going to get in touch with our council?"

I nodded. "Yeah, that's what they told us. I guess we'll find out more tomorrow."

She walked towards me. "Aria, how is it going with your scriptures? Do you know what you're going to do? You know that I'll never turn my back on you. No matter what. I could never do what Mom did to Aunt Violet."

I hugged her. "Thanks. I'm doing good. I've learned both scriptures and I think I know what I'll choose. Thank you for not being such a bitch about things."

Alexia laughed as she pushed me away. "Whatever. I guess we better get to bed. I feel like we're going to have some long days ahead of us, don't you?"

I smiled at my sister. "Yeah, I'm sure we are. Good night, sis."

She stuck her tongue out at me. "Night, biatch."

The second my sister walked out of the room I got my phone. I clicked on Ethan's number and sent him a text. "Hey, I'm on my way to the school—alone."

Chapter Nineteen

I snuck out of my house through my window and I almost got myself caught by hitting the trash-can on my way down. *Real smooth Aria, real smooth.*

I got my bicycle out of the garage and headed towards the school.

As I got closer, my nerves started getting the best of me. Before I got directly in front of the building, I parked my bike on the side of the empty school.

I texted Grayson. "I'm here. I'm not feeling too good. I think I may throw up. Hope you're close by—A."

I put my phone in my jacket pocket and walked towards the Dark building.

The closer I got to the school, the sicker I felt. I leaned over and started to gag. I looked up and saw that Ethan was standing directly in front of me.

He handed me a bottle of water. "Hey, cuz. Feeling okay?"

I took the bottle from him and drank some. "I'm fine, thanks."

He looked at me with his glowing violet eyes. "If you say so. I'm surprised you actually came alone. I for sure thought you'd have that Treble boy with you."

I glared at him. "Um, why would you think that?"

He laughed. "Let's be real, Aria. I know you two are dating. His presence around you is...very strong. He's made it clear that you are his."

I took another drink of water. "I'm not anyone's, so whatever. What do you want, Ethan? Why am I meeting you here this late?"

He looked around to make sure no one was close by. "Let's go inside. I don't think it's safe for us to talk out here."

I pushed him. "Ethan, quit playing games. Why am I here? How is it not safe to talk in front of our school? Why couldn't you just talk to me over the phone?"

My cousin kept his eyes wandering into the Darkness around our school. "Aria, I know you know what my mom did. I also know you know who she's working with, right?"

I shook my head. "What are you talking about?"

He grabbed my arm. "Don't be silly! I know you know about my mom working with him."

I pulled my arm away from him. "Who are you talking about? Get to the point, Ethan! I have had a long day and I'm over it. I need to get home and get some rest."

He sighed. "Aria, my mom is going crazy! I don't even want to be around her. I don't know what to do! She can't ever find out that I met with you tonight."

I looked at him, warily. "Okay, I know she's working with Sebastian. How is that even possible? How did she find him? Where is she now?"

He leaned in closer to me. "Can we please go inside and talk? I just have a bad feeling right now."

I looked around and then signaled for him to take the lead towards the school. We walked into the building, which for some reason was not locked. I stared at him as he locked the door.

He laughed menacingly. "What? I didn't break in or anything. I found this key." He held a bronze key in front of me.

Before he could put the key back into his pocket, we saw a bright yellow Light flash outside.

He whispered, "Aria, get down! It's Sebastian's trackers. They're looking for me, I'm sure."

I squatted next to him and whispered back, "What the hell do you mean, Sebastian's trackers are looking for you?"

He looked at me and put his finger over his mouth, signaling for me to quit talking.

We both sat there quietly, and saw that the blinding Lights were flooding our Dark school from the outside, in.

After a few minutes, Ethan slowly stood up and looked out the window. He looked down at me. "Okay, we're in the clear."

He helped me stand up as I dusted my hands on my jeans. "What the hell was that about?"

Ethan's hands were shaking. "Aria, when we found your family here, my mom told me that we were going to meet you all and that it would be okay. I was excited to meet my family."

I looked at him, confused. He went on, "After a day of being here my mom told me that you all were Light and that's why I couldn't meet any of you. She then said if I went to your school, we could technically talk because you haven't been through your Reckoning."

He sat on the floor, against some lockers now. "Another few days went on and my mom started talking about how I needed to get you on 'our side'. She kept talking to me about getting you to turn Dark and manipulating you."

He looked at me and pointed at the ground next to him. I sat down as he cleared his throat.

"Cuz, I am a Dark Fae. I am a Dark because that's all I've ever known. I'm not a bad person. I've done bad things, but if you knew my mom...If you knew her, you'd know why."

I put my hand on his. "Ethan, I'm sorry. I'm sorry that your mom has forced you to do things you haven't wanted to do. Why are you telling me all this?"

His eyes lost all their violet glow before he answered me. "I'm telling you this, because I know what she has planned for you. I'm telling you this because I'm afraid that if she gets what she wants, she'll really be unstoppable."

I looked at his sad eyes and asked, "What does Sebastian Harper have to do with any of this?"

He looked into my eyes and with a shaky voice, he said, "They're going to turn you into their most valuable weapon against the Light Fae."

Chapter Twenty

I sat there, stunned by what I had just heard. What the hell did he mean that they want to use me as a weapon? I asked, "Ethan, why do you think they're trying to use me? What makes you think that I would ever agree to their little plan anyways?"

Ethan looked at me with his dimmed eyes. "Aria, believe me. They can be *very* convincing. They can probably make you do things that you wouldn't ever dare to do."

I shook my head. "I don't think that they'd ever be able to get to me. I know what Violet did to our grandparents, do you?"

He went from staring into my eyes to looking at the ground. "Yeah, I know what she did."

I forced him to look at me again. "Ethan, why would your mom do that? She killed our grandparents! How could you choose to go Dark after she did something so horrendous?"

His eyes lit up with anger. "I already told you, my mother can be very convincing. She gets what she wants, no questions asked. If someone questions her, they won't be around too long after."

I put my hand on his shoulder. "Why do they want me to become their weapon? The Light and Dark Fae have been co-existing with our new laws forever now."

He moved my hand from his shoulder and sighed. "There are some Dark Fae who want to eradicate the Light. Sebastian has a strong following and when word gets out that he's back, things are going to get really bad, really quick."

My phone started ringing. I looked at Ethan as he nodded at me. "Go ahead, answer your phone. I'm sure your boyfriend is worried about you."

I picked up the phone. Grayson's worried voice came through the other end. "Aria, are you okay? Where are you? I couldn't stay away. We're outside of the school but I can't see you anywhere."

I cleared my throat. "I am fine. We're inside of the school."

He grunted. "Where in the school? I'm coming in, Briar and Cayne will wait outside."

I looked at my cousin. "Is it okay if Grayson comes in? I think you should tell him what you're telling me."

Ethan's eyes lit up again. "Aria, do you trust him?"

I stared at my phone and then back at him. "Yes, I do. You can too."

He nodded and I gave Grayson the okay. "Meet us by the gym. We'll let you in there. Tell Cayne and Briar to wait in their car. I don't think it's safe for them to wait outside."

Grayson agreed and as I stared outside the windows by the gym, I saw him running towards the building. I opened the gym door for him as he approached us. He ran in and hugged me. "I was so worried. I'm sorry I couldn't stay away."

Ethan walked up to us. "I'm very surprised that you kept your promise, cousin."

I gave him an ugly stare-down. "Really? I told you I'd come alone, so I did. Grayson didn't think it was smart of me to come alone, but I didn't care. To be honest, I'm kind of glad I did come."

Grayson grabbed my hand. I kept going, "Ethan, tell Grayson what you've told me."

Ethan's violet glow faded again as he spoke. "My mom and Sebastian are working together. They've been trying to use me to get to Aria. They want her to turn Dark so they can use her as a weapon to eliminate all of the Light Fae. They believe that once the Light Fae are gone, we will be able to absorb their powers and become the higher beings in this world. They want to get rid of the Light Fae and quit hiding from the humans."

Grayson whispered, "They want the humans to serve us again, right?"

I looked at him confused as Ethan nodded in agreement. I asked, "They want the mundanes to be our servants? I thought that was just a rumor. I didn't know that mundanes were actually servants at one time."

Ethan went on, "They were our slaves until Sebastian disappeared. The Light Fae decided to go into hiding as the Dark followed in their footsteps. They all then came up with the ideas of councils and the Royals. They govern the Fae to make sure we stay hidden from the mundanes."

Grayson looked at me as he asked Ethan, "Why do they want to use Aria as a weapon? What could she do for them that they can't do on their own?"

Ethan's eyes stayed dim as he answered Grayson nervously. "Aria is a born natural."

He spoke to me now, "You're destined to be one of the most powerful Fae of all time. If you're Light, you'll go on to do great things for all of our kind. If you go Dark, things will be a little less good for some of us...well, most of us."

Chapter Twenty-One

I challenged my cousin. "How in the hell do they know what I'm destined to become? How do they know I'm a natural-born? I haven't been through my Reckoning yet!"

My cousin looked at Grayson and then laughed. "You know too, don't you?"

I turned my attention to Grayson who looked at the ground. I demanded, "Grayson, what is he saying?"

Grayson whispered, "Yes, I just found out you're a natural-born."

I stepped away from him. "How in the hell do you know? How is that even possible?"

Ethan laughed again, "And you trust him? He's a joke. I'm telling you everything he's known and has hidden from you. Go on Grayson. Tell her how you know."

Grayson's eyes lit up violet with frustration. "Ethan, shut up. You're making it seem like I've known this whole time."

He turned his attention to me again. "Aria, I just found out the other day."

He reached for my hand as I pulled it away. "Don't touch me."

His eyes stayed lit up, although I could see a bit of sadness in them now. "I swear to you that I only found out when you were going over the Dark scriptures with me. I don't think Sebastian or Violet knows this, but you are a natural-born. Your Reckoning will not be the same as everyone else's."

Ethan looked at the both of us as he spoke. "How will her Reckoning be any different? She'll have to choose Light or Dark."

Grayson responded, "She will choose, but she doesn't have to wait until her Reckoning to use her natural powers. I think that's why Sebastian is really trying to get to you. He knows that you're some how even stronger than Violet. If you go Light, you will be the most dangerous Fae to him. You will be able to ruin everything he's hoping to accomplish."

I sank back to the ground. "I don't have any powers."

Grayson sat next to me. "You do. You have some of the most powerful abilities we'll ever see. You started feeling sick on your way here, right?"

I nodded as I saw Ethan sit across from us. Grayson went on, "Cayne says that you were feeling sick because you could feel the danger that was close by. Before I called you, Briar and Cayne were scouting the area and saw that Sebastian had trackers and elementals on your tail. They were pretty much trying to kidnap you. Your natural defenses kicked in and you deterred them."

I looked at him as his violet glow started to fade from his eyes. "What do you mean, I deterred them?"

Ethan spoke from across the hall. "You have a natural defense. You're able to throw trackers off your trail. That explains why I went on a wild-goose chase when I first moved here. It took me a lot longer to find you then my mom wanted. I only found you because I found Alexia and followed her. I was unable to pick up on your imprint."

Grayson nodded and picked up my hand. "Aria, you can throw trackers off, you can avoid an elemental's touch and that's just the surface of what we think you are capable of."

Ethan stood up and asked, "Do you think that she can manipulate imprints?"

Grayson went from looking at me to looking at my cousin. He nodded.

I gasped. "How is that possible? I haven't ever tried."

Grayson quietly answered me, "Cayne left some 'traps' for you and left his imprint. As you rode your bike here, the sicker you felt, the more your powers kicked in. You completely erased your imprint and Cayne's. Briar couldn't believe it and neither could I."

I asked, "I don't understand why I felt so sick, though? Do all naturals feel like this when they're using their powers?"

Ethan answered me, "My mom told me she got violently ill right before her full powers became intact. She was really sick until the night she killed our grandparents."

Grayson's phone rang when Ethan finished his sentence. It took him a minute to answer but when he did, I heard Cayne shouting from the other end. "Grayson, you all need to get out of there, now!"

We all jumped up as Grayson asked, "Cayne, what is it? What's going on?"

Cayne was on speaker-phone now. "Violet's here. We saw her walking towards the school. She has a tracker with her."

I looked at Ethan as he looked outside the window. He murmured, "Crap. Grayson, your brother's right, my mom is here and she looks pissed."

I spoke up, "We need to get out of here, let's go through the cafeteria. We can meet Cayne and Briar at the back of the school".

We ran to the back of the school where Cayne and Briar were waiting in their SUV. We all jumped in as Grayson shouted, "Holy shit!"

I turned to him. "What's going on? Are you okay?"

I looked out the window and saw what had shocked him. Violet was standing outside the school's door. Her eyes had a menacing glow to them. Her hands were in the air and bright yellow Lights ran from her palms to the sky.

Cayne shouted at Briar, "Hurry up and drive! She's nuts and is gonna try to kill us!"

Ethan stayed quiet for a minute and when we finally pulled away from the school, he spoke. "My mom knows I'm with you all. I can't go back home now. I don't know what I'm going to do."

I put my hand on his. "We will figure something out, okay?"

His eyes lit up with sadness and removed my hand from his. Grayson spoke, "You can stay with us until we figure this all out. Now that I know your mom is a full-on psychopath, we can't send you back with her."

Cayne turned around from the front seat and asked, "Do you think she'd actually hurt you?"

Ethan huffed. "Nah, she wouldn't hurt me. She'd probably kill me."

Briar was still trying to catch his breath from the excitement of everything that had just happened. He asked, "Are you sure that she knows you're with us?"

Ethan looked at me and then nodded. "Yeah, I'm sure she knows I came to tell Aria everything I know."

He leaned into his seat and went on, "To be honest, when I first moved here, I was onboard with my mom's plan. I thought getting Aria to join the Dark side would be a great idea."

He met my eyes. "After meeting you at the school and seeing you, I just couldn't go through with it anymore."

He sat up now, positioning himself close to Grayson. "I'm ready to talk to your parents. I need them to know everything that's going to happen."

As we pulled onto my street, my heart jolted. Grayson looked at me. "Aria, what's wrong?"

I pointed at all the SUVs that were parked in front of my house. The Lights in the living room were on and I saw a bunch of Dark Fae, in suits. They were all standing outside my house and around the SUVs.

Grayson, Briar and Cayne mumbled, "Shit has hit the fan" in unison.

Ethan looked through the front window and laughed. "Could this night get any worse? What the hell is going on in the universe tonight?"

Briar parked the vehicle across the street from my house and before any of us could open a door, the Fae in suits had surrounded us. One of the Fae, who had Darker skin, spoke to Cayne. "Sir, your parents are inside. They need all of you to report to the living area, immediately."

Briar asked, "Joshua, what the hell is going on? Why are our parents here?"

Joshua shook his head and responded, "I am not authorized to release any information to you, sir. We will park your vehicle. Please go into the Whitelace's home."

We all looked at each other as Grayson spoke, "Let's get this crap over with. Are you all ready?"

We nodded and followed Joshua into my home. We walked inside and my mom ran over to me and hugged me, her eyes tear-filled. "Aria, we were so worried about you! Your dad went into your room earlier and realized you were gone. We called the Trebles and they informed us that Grayson was also missing."

Mrs. Treble spoke, "At first we were sure you all were just being teenagers and would eventually end up back at home. However, we then had reports of Violet Whitelace heading towards your school. We sent patrols there but they were unable to gain access to your school's parking lot. All of the trees around your school were uprooted and blocked the only entrance."

We all looked at each other, confused. Grayson spoke, "We were able to get into the parking lot just fine. We barely made it out, though."

Mr. Treble asked, "Was Violet there? Are you all okay?"

Before any of us could respond, my dad asked, "What is he doing here?"

We all turned our attention to Ethan who was standing at the front door.

Chapter Twenty-Two

Ethan's eyes immediately lit up. He didn't answer my dad so my mom asked, "What are you doing here, Ethan Whitelace?"

I went to Ethan and stood by his side. I said, "Ethan is here because I trust him. He has nowhere else to go. Violet knows that he's told me everything."

Mr. Treble asked, "What do you mean he told you everything? What exactly did he tell you, Aria?"

I was about to start talking but Ethan cut me off. "I told her my mom's plan. She is working with Sebastian and they want to use Aria to eradicate the Light Fae."

My mom gasped. My dad asked, "And why do you all of a sudden feel like doing the right thing? You're a Dark…"

His sentence trailed off as Mr. Treble cleared his throat. "With all due respect, Mr. Whitelace, I think we should hear the boy out. After all, you have been to our home. Hopefully you know that not all Dark Fae are bad."

My mom took my dad's hand. "Liam, if Aria trusts him, I think we should too."

My dad sighed and signaled for us to join them in the living area. Ethan stood in place for another minute before walking towards the group.

Ethan's eyes dimmed and I saw that tears were now running down his face. Cherise Treble hurried to him and wrapped her arms around him. "Now, now sweetie. It's going to be okay."

Ethan mumbled, "No, it's not. You don't know my mother. She is going to kill me."

He pulled away from Grayson's mom, adding, "I was going to choose Light during my Reckoning. I didn't want to become what she was. My mom forced me to go Dark. I never had a choice. That's what Sebastian and her want. They want the ability to choose between Light and Dark to be non-existent. They think the Light's powers are useless. And by ridding the world of them, we'll be able to absorb their energy."

We were all silent as Mrs. Treble asked, "How long have you known that your mom was working with Sebastian Harper?"

Ethan responded, "I've known Sebastian my entire life. I didn't know exactly who he was until we moved here. My mom wanted me to get close to Aria so I could persuade her to choose the Dark. After meeting Aria and seeing how she acted around her friends at school, I saw that her soul is clearly Light."

Grayson made eye contact with me as Cayne spoke. "Don't you all think it's wise to tell everyone what we learned about Aria this evening?"

My dad asked, "What exactly did you all learn about my daughter?"

My mom put her hand on my dad's arm to calm him down. His eyes were lit up a blue-ish gray. Ethan answered, "Aria is a natural-born."

The room was filled with noise as he finished his sentence. My mom's eyes were now matching my dad's. I looked at the Trebles and saw all violet eyes. They were all shouting and I could barely make anything out. I screamed out, "Enough!"

Everyone fell silent. My mom held onto my dad tightly. They were both crying. Grayson slowly walked closer to me. "Aria, calm down."

I looked at him, confused. "What are you talking about? I'm okay."

He turned his focus to my hands and I looked down. What the hell was that? I screamed out, "Oh my God! What's happening to me?"

My hands and arms had turned to an aqua color. There were specks of violets and greens sparkling off my skin. I cried out, "Mom, Dad, what's happening? What is this?"

My parents continued crying as Mr. Treble spoke. "Aria, this is a sign that your powers have fully activated. You are a natural-born. You are a very unique natural-born."

I sunk to the floor. "That's impossible. I haven't been through my Reckoning. I still have a few more months…"

Mrs. Treble walked over to me. "Sweetie, do you know that Reckonings only started after the Fae war?"

I nodded as Cayne joined us. "Aria, the original Faes didn't go through Reckonings. They just were what they were. A natural creation on this planet. Just like Mundanes. Mundanes are what they are. They don't go through a Reckoning to become an adult. I mean, sure, they go through puberty, but that isn't like a Reckoning."

Grayson asked, "What are you all saying? Why's this happening to Aria? Natural Faes still go through their Reckoning."

Briar answered, "I think what they're saying is that Aria will have to choose Light or Dark sooner than she'd like."

He turned his attention to me now. "Aria, it looks like you will not go through a Reckoning. It's obvious that your powers are fully intact."

My mom wiped the tears from her face. "Baby, come here."

I ran to her and she hugged me so tight, I could barely breathe. My dad joined the hug. He whispered, "It's going to be okay, baby. We are here for you."

I glanced back towards the Trebles. "Will my skin stay like this?"

Cayne answered me, "No, but it seems likely that it will turn to this when you use your powers."

Grayson asked, "What kind of powers does she have? We know she has a natural defense. How many other powers could she have?"

Cayne looked at us before he answered. "We won't know until she experiments with all of them."

He took my hands and pulled me from my parents. "Aria, you're going to start going through a lot of emotions. It's important that you follow the direction your mind needs you to."

My dad added, "Aria, you won't be doing this alone. Your mother and I are here for you."

Alexia's voice came to us and we all turned to see her coming down the stairs. "I'm here for you too, sis."

I ran over to Alexia with tears in my eyes. She hugged me tightly and cried, "Aria, you're a natural-born?"

I nodded and kept my hold on her as we walked back to the living area. I pulled my head from our embrace and introduced her to everyone.

Cayne's eyes lit up when he shook Alexia's hand. "It's a pleasure to meet you, Alexia Whitelace."

My sister blushed. "It's nice to meet you, too, Cayne Treble."

My dad cleared his throat. "It's getting late. I think we should call it a night."

Mr. Treble agreed. "Why don't you all come over for brunch tomorrow? I think we have a lot to discuss."

My parents looked at each other. My mom answered, "We will have to inform our council in the morning. I will call you all once we've received their approval."

Cherise smiled. "That's wonderful, we'll see you all tomorrow."

My parents started to escort the Trebles out when my mom asked, "What are we going to do with Ethan?"

Ethan looked at me, his eyes filled with a heavy sadness. My dad met our stare. "Ethan, why don't you stay with the Trebles tonight? We will meet with the council in the morning and tell them about your situation. Perhaps, if it's okay with them, you can stay with us?"

Ethan's eyes lit up with happiness. "Really? That'd be great. Thank you Mr. Whitelace."

My dad patted Ethan's back. "Call me Uncle Liam. Have a good night, Ethan."

Chapter Twenty-Three

The next morning, my parents let me sleep in until almost noon. Grayson woke me up when he called my cellphone. I answered, "H-hello?"

I could feel him grinning on the other side of the phone. "Well, good morning sleepyhead! You do know it's almost noon, right?"

I pulled the phone away from my face to check the time. Man, I must have been really tired. I giggled, "Yeah, I guess I was exhausted. How did last night go with Ethan?"

Grayson stayed quiet for a second before answering me. "It was interesting. I couldn't sleep because I felt like I needed to keep an eye on him. He had a room down the hall from me, but slept on my floor. I guess he's not as tough as he comes off."

I laughed again and asked, "Where is he? I'm really worried about him. I thought about what he said last night and he's probably right. His mom will kill him if she gets a hold of him."

Grayson sighed. "Yeah, you're right. I know she will. He's downstairs with Briar and Cayne. They're doing some research on Sebastian and a few other natural-born Fae. We're all trying to get to the bottom of what happened to you last night. How are you feeling, Aria?"

I looked at my hands to make sure the blue, green and violet sparkles were gone. "Oh, okay. I'm doing fine. I heard my parents talking about it this morning when I went to get some water. I don't think they've ever heard of anything like this either."

He asked, "Aria, last night when your skin turned, how were you feeling?"

I thought for a couple of seconds. "Hm, I know that at first I was annoyed."

Grayson asked softly, "Is that it?"

I thought for a moment. "Um, I think so."

Grayson shouted, "Cayne, Briar, get ready we need to go to Aria's."

I rolled my eyes. "What happened? Why do you all need to come over here? I thought that we were going to head over for brunch. My parents got the green Light from our council."

He let out a nervous laugh. "My dad is meeting with your council privately and I think we need to put our heads together with your parents. Maybe between all of us, we'll be able to figure out what happened to you last night."

I sighed. "Okay, I'll see you in a bit."

As I hung up the phone, Alexia walked into the room. "Hey, sis. How are you feeling? I brought you come coffee."

I reached out for the coffee cup. "Ah, thank you. I'm okay. I'm still a bit tired."

She sat next to me on the bed. "I bet. Last night was kind of insane, huh?"

I nodded. "Yeah, you could definitely say that."

She chuckled. "Mom and Dad are going to drop Declan off at his friend's house for the weekend. Maybe they don't want him to be around until they know exactly what happened."

I sighed. "Yeah, that's probably the best idea. Speaking of that, Grayson and his brothers are on their way here."

Alexia blushed. "Oh, really? I should probably get decent then, huh?"

I rolled my eyes. "Um, I guess? Why are you blushing?"

She punched me. "Don't be such a bitch, Aria. I mean, why didn't you ever tell me that Grayson's family is so attractive? His mom is beautiful. His dad...his dad could be a Greek God. And then Cayne and Briar...uh, I need to hurry up and go get ready."

She stood up and looked at herself in the mirror. "Ugh, I feel extra fat today."

I laughed. "Just today?"

She threw a brush at me as she walked out of my room. "Lose the attitude, girl. You should probably do something about your mess of a look, too."

I leaned over to look at my hair in the mirror. Yikes, she was right! I stood up and started to get ready. My cellphone rang again. I answered it. "Hello?"

After a couple of seconds with no response, I looked at the caller ID. Hmm, an unknown number. I sighed. "Hello? Who is this? Who are you looking for?"

When she spoke, chills went up my spine. "Aria, it's your aunt. How are you?"

I felt a burning sensation run from my chest through the rest of my body. I stayed quiet until she spoke again. "How is my dear, dear son? I hope he's well."

I spit out. "What the hell do you want? How did you get my number?"

Violet laughed. "Watch your tone with me, young lady. That mouth of yours could get you in a whole lot of trouble."

I rolled my eyes. "I'm not scared of you. Now, answer me. How in the hell did you get my number?"

The burning sensation now filled my body. I felt my hands shaking. I looked at my reflection in the mirror and saw that my body was covered with the different like the night before. Violet broke my concentration with a groan. "I see your powers have come in full force, huh? How does it feel? Can you feel the Darkness running through your veins? That burning sensation you are feeling, let it take you over. It is the best thing for you."

I stopped looking at myself in the mirror and turned my attention back to our conversation. "Violet, what do you want? You're wasting my time."

Violet cleared her throat before she answered me. "I want my son to come home. I need you to tell him that his mother forgives him for his temporary lapse into stupidity."

I started getting dressed as the conversation went on. I put my phone on speaker and threw a shoe into the hall, hoping I'd get someone's attention.

Thankfully, it worked. Alexia walked into the room. "Aria, what the he—"

She looked at me and then at my cellphone. Her eyes lit up a blue-ish gray.

Violet kept talking, "Aria, did you hear what I said? You need to quit being so rude. The next time I see you, remind me to teach you some manners."

I cut her off. "Violet, I will tell Ethan you called. I will not tell him to go back to you. You're a psychotic bitch. You tried to kill us last night."

She let out an eerie laugh. "You foolish girl. I didn't try to kill any of you. If I had, one of you would be dead. I guess you could say, I tried to get your attention. Did it work, dear?"

I put my hair in a ponytail while Alexia was texting someone, furiously. I sat on my bed. "I'm done with this conversation, Violet. The next time we see each other, please make sure you remind me to show you who the strongest Whiteface really is. Oh, and can you tell Sebastian to quit hiding? Talk to you later."

I hung up the phone and Alexia looked at me with her mouth fully open. I laughed. "Why are you looking at me like that? Who were you texting?"

She smiled at me. "Okay, let's see. Your skin looks totally amazing and you just told Violet off. Way to go, sis!"

I rolled my eyes and stood up from the bed. "Whatever. Who were you texting?"

She headed towards the hallway. "I was texting Mom and Dad. They're on their way back home."

I nodded as our doorbell rang. Alexia squealed, "I think the Treble boys are here!"

Chapter Twenty-Four

Alexia and I ran down the stairs to answer the door. Grayson stood in front of his two brothers and Ethan. As the door fully opened, he lunged at me with open arms. He pulled back a little as everyone made their way into the house. He asked, "Did something happen?"

Alexia sarcastically asked, "Why in the world would you ask a question like that?"

Cayne and Briar's eyes lit up. Ethan stood in front of me now. "Aria, is everything okay?"

I felt the familiar burning sensation running through my body again. I spoke through my gritted teeth. "Your mother called."

Ethan touched my arm. "You've got to calm down Aria."

Grayson pushed past Ethan. "Aria, listen to me. You have got to calm down. Look at your hands."

I looked down at my hands. I saw the blues, greens and purples blending together. They were starting to let of a bright sparkling glow. I looked up at Grayson and Ethan. "What's happening to me?"

Cayne answered me. "Your powers are taking over, Aria. I know you don't want to hear this, but you're channeling a lot of Dark right now. Please, try to calm down."

I closed my eyes and felt warm tears fall on my cheek. Alexia put her hand on my back and immediately withdrew it. "Ouch, Aria, you burned me!"

I opened my eyes and felt the tears flow more quickly. "I'm so sorry, Alexia. I don't know what's happening."

Briar spoke, "You've got to listen to us. Cayne's right, you are channeling a lot of Dark powers. We can talk about it when your parents get here, just calm down."

Grayson leaned in and kissed me before I could say anything else. The moment his lips touched mine, the burning sensation dissipated. I felt his cool, soft lips on mine. The coolness from his lips sent shivers up and down my entire body. The tears that were falling from my eyes felt like icicles. Grayson pulled away from me after a couple of minutes. "Whoa!"

I opened my eyes and looked down at my hands. They were normal again. I turned back to Alexia who was being comforted by Cayne. She gave me a half-smile. "Don't worry about me, it's just a small burn."

I winced. "I'm sorry, Alexia."

She nodded. "I know, it's okay, sis."

I turned my attention back to Grayson. "What is happening to me?"

It took a couple of seconds for him to respond. Briar hit him on his arm. "Bro, are you alright?"

Grayson looked at his brothers and then at me. "Aria, you were channeling some Light powers just now. Your inner Light shut off the Dark you were projecting just a few minutes ago."

Cayne murmured, "That's impossible."

As if on cue, my parents walked into the house.

Chapter Twenty-Five

My mom must have felt the tension because she immediately ran to me. "Aria, baby, are you okay? What's going on?"

I embraced her in a hug and assured her that I was fine. "I'm doing okay, Mom. The guys came over to talk about some theories they've come up with."

She pulled away from me as my dad walked into our house. She looked up at him. "Honey, call the council. One of the members needs to be here for this."

My dad nodded and picked up his cellphone. "We have a few members from the Royal family here. Would you all like to send someone to witness our conversation?"

We all looked at him, waiting for his response. "Oh? Okay. We will call you immediately after. Thank you."

He hung up the phone and then looked at all of us. "The council feels like we have been very forthcoming already. They trust our intentions with the Trebles."

Grayson and I both let out a sigh of relief. Cayne spoke now, "Mr. and Mrs. Whitelace, we have been up all night researching different kinds of natural-born Faes."

My mom signaled for us to sit in the living room as Briar added, "We didn't find anything too new. We already know that Aria has a natural defense power."

He looked at me and then went on, "Does someone want to tell them about what just happened?"

Grayson grabbed my hand as he took the seat next to me. "Aria was visibly upset because Violet reached out to her before we got here and…"

My dad cut him off mid-sentence. "What do you mean, Violet reached out to her?"

My parents both asked me, "Did she call you? What did she say?"

Grayson answered them before I had the chance to. "We can get to that in a second. That's not really the most important thing right now."

My mom looked at him, confused. "Well, okay. What is it then? What happened?"

He cleared his throat and squeezed my hands a little tighter. "Aria was radiating a lot of Dark powers...and then I sort of kissed her."

I looked at my parents as both of their eyes lit up. My dad asked, "Why are you telling us this?"

Grayson started to blush as he released my hands to wipe his sweaty palms on his jeans. "Because when I kissed her, trying to calm her down, she then started projecting a Light defensive power."

My parents looked at each other and then at me. My mom spoke, "That's impossible...that hasn't happened since..."

Her voice trailed off as Cayne finished her sentence. "...it hasn't happened since the original Fae."

Chapter Twenty-Six

My parents stayed quiet, tears running down both their faces. Ethan stood up from the sofa and sat on the floor in front of them. "Uncle Liam, Adalyn, we don't know what any of this means. Aria is obviously not going through a Reckoning. But, she still has to choose either Light or Dark. There's still that."

My dad's worried eyes looked at me as he answered my cousin. "I know she'll have to choose. We just don't know what to do for her until that day comes."

My mom changed the subject and asked, "What did Violet want, Aria?"

I looked at my cousin, with saddened eyes as I answered her. "She wants Ethan to go home."

Ethan's head jerked towards me. "Does she think I'm stupid? She tried to kill me! She tried to kill us!"

I looked down as I went on, "She said that if she had wanted us dead, then one of us would be dead by now."

Alexia spoke up now. "Aria totally went into bitchy survival mode. She told her off alright."

My parents looked at Alexia, disapprovingly and confused. My dad asked me, "What is your sister talking about?"

I stared at my nails, chipping at the polish without thinking what I was doing. "Um, I kind of told Violet that she needed to tell Sebastian to quit hiding from all of us. Oh and there was this kind of challenge that came out of nowhere…"

My voice got quiet as my mom protested. "Aria Whitelace, what challenge? What are you talking about?"

I kept fidgeting with my fingernails. "Um, I told her that the next time I see her, she needed to remind me to show her who the strongest Whitelace really was."

Ethan let out a loud laugh. "Way to go, cuz! You're a total badass!"

Alexia chimed in, "I know, right?"

Grayson's eyes lit up with disapproval. "Aria, why would you challenge Violet? You've seen what she's capable of."

I put my hands back down at my sides as I answered him. "I know, I've seen what she's capable of. But, she hasn't seen what I'm capable of. And I've got the strangest feeling that I'm a bit stronger than she is."

Cayne, of course, was the first to bring me back down to Earth. "No offense, Aria, but you don't even know how strong you are. None of us know what you're capable of. None of us know what type of natural-born you are. We don't know what powers you'll be able to use. We don't know if you'll have a connection with the elements, the spirit realm, or if you'll just be a healer."

I huffed. "Um, we already know that I've got the natural defense down. And the whole element thing, what do you think the burning sensation is? When I get angry or scared, I start to feel it run through my body. And when Grayson and I first touched, we both felt it."

I looked at Grayson for confirmation. "Right? Tell them…"

Grayson nodded. "Aria, I agree with my brother. We don't know what you're capable of. You have to be able to control all your powers, in order to say you're a truly strong, natural-born."

Briar spoke from the other side of the room. "And then there's the whole, will-you-go-Dark or will-you-go-Light argument. Eventually, you will have to choose. If your powers are starting to come through to you, so you'll probably have to make your choice soon."

I looked at everyone in the room. I was the only Fae here who had not been through a Reckoning. I was the only Fae in here that had not chosen a side. I asked, "How will I know when it's time for me to choose?"

Everyone looked at one another before anyone answered my question. Grayson responded, "It is an unforgettable, painful experience. I can tell you that it will happen on a blood moon. I can also tell you, from my experience, that it feels as if your soul is getting violently ripped out of your body."

I felt fearful tears running down my warm face. Grayson went on, "Your body will be lifted towards the blood moon until you allow your heart to choose what you want. The pain you'll be feeling will block you from choosing what you want with your mind. The blood moon only takes answers from the heart, hence the ripping sensation."

I looked at Alexia. "Did you feel that pain?"

Alexia looked at my parents and then back at me. "Aria, Grayson is telling you the exact truth. He's explaining it to you better than I ever could. It will happen on a blood moon and it will totally feel as if your soul is being ripped out of your body."

I turned to my parents and then to Cayne and Briar. "When is the next blood moon?"

No one answered me. I shouted, "When is the next blood moon, dammit?"

Ethan whispered, "It's in eleven days."

Chapter Twenty-Seven

I started to nervously pace around the room as everyone else remained mute. "So you're telling me that I will have to choose the Light or Dark side, in less than two weeks? In less than two weeks I will have to know how to control all these unknown powers that some greater being has just given to me?"

I felt the now-familiar burning sensation begin to tingle in my palms. I closed my eyes and took a couple of deep breaths to calm myself.

Grayson's soft voice came through to me. "Aria, you're amazing."

I opened my eyes and saw that he was standing in front of me. He grabbed my hand and lifted it to his face. He smiled at me as he kissed my palm. "You did it. You stopped the Darkness before it could take you over."

I smiled back at him. "I did do it, huh?"

I leaned into him and kissed his amazingly soft lips. His vibrating cellphone interrupted the intimate moment before my parents could. He answered it on speaker-phone. "Hello? Mom? What's going on? You're on speaker."

Mrs. Treble's strained voice came through. "I think you all should come to the house, now."

Cayne and Briar were at our sides now. "What happened?"

Mr. Treble joined the conversation. "We just got a video message from Violet Whitelace."

Everyone's eyes were now lit up with anxiety. Grayson asked, "What did she say?"

Mrs. Treble answered, "She didn't say anything, really. She just introduced us to someone. I really think you all should just come home, right now."

Briar pushed on. "Mom, we will be there shortly. Who did she introduce you to?"

Mr. Treble answered for his wife. "She introduced us to Sebastian Harper. He is alive and he wants his throne back."

My family and I followed the Trebles back to their home. My parents were frantically calling council members on the way. My mom looked at my dad in between calls. "Do you think it's true? Do you think that it is actually Sebastian Harper? Do you think he'd actually work with my sister?"

My dad's shoulders tensed up. "I hope not Adalyn. We will find out soon enough. What did the others say when you told them?"

My mom was texting someone when she looked up. "They want us to verify the video message and then they will probably send someone to the Trebles' home."

My dad nodded. "That's probably best."

As my dad parked our car in the driveway, Alexia leaned over and whispered to me. "What do you think is going to happen if Sebastian is back? We don't have a Light Fae leader since Lucas is still moving." She unbuckled her seat belt and continued, "Who's going to fight him?"

My mom answered for me. "Alexia, we will cross that bridge when we get there. Let's get this out of the way first."

I looked out of my window and saw Grayson standing in front of it. He smiled at me as he opened the door. "Are you okay?"

I hugged him as we started walking into his home. "Yeah, I'm kind of anxious. I've got a bad feeling about this." I lowered my voice to a whisper. "I don't think Violet is pulling our strings. I think it is actually Sebastian."

He looked at me and nodded. "I think so, too."

We made our way into the Trebles' home and towards their living area. As I stepped into the room, I saw ten Dark Fae surrounding Mr. and Mrs. Treble. They were all speaking fast, with worry in their voices.

I heard one of them ask, "Where should we go looking first?"

Mr. Treble waved him off as he greeted my parents. "Liam, Adalyn, welcome back to our home. Have a seat and we'll play the video for you all."

I shook Braden's hand and hugged Cherise as I sat next to Grayson. He grabbed my hand

and squeezed it as his parents hit 'play' on the video message.

Violet appeared on the projector screen, her eyes filled with a cruel violet color. She cleared her throat before speaking. "Mr. and Mrs. Treble, consider this your warning. You will immediately turn your powers over to the True One. You are no longer the Royal family of the Dark Fae. Leave quietly if you value your lives."

She let out an eerie chuckle and continued, "You may be wondering who the True One is, and let me be the one to confirm your suspicions. Let me introduce you to my King, *your* King, Sebastian Harper."

A Dark-skinned man with spiky hair appeared on the screen now. His eyes were a deep plum and had a glow to them that I had never seen before. It was a mixture of a violet and blue.

He smiled, showing off his perfect teeth. "Hello, my children. I hope you have been keeping my home nice and cozy. Let me introduce myself to any of you who may not know me. I am Sebastian Harper. I am the original Fae and I am back. I will annihilate all Light Fae and any Dark who stand in my way.

Consider this my warning, either step down and join me in the fight that is to come, or stand in the way and get killed."

Chapter Twenty-Eight

The screen went black and chaos ensued. There were screams of anger coming from every corner of the room. Grayson stood as I did and we shouted in unison, "Enough!"

Everyone fell quiet and as I opened my eyes and started to focus on the Fae around me, I saw why.

Grayson and I had our hands in the air and there was a bright orb surrounding our bodies. The orb had different shades of blue, green, and purple. I looked at Grayson, who still had his eyes shut, and saw that he was violently shaking.

I put my hand down and pulled it away from his. He opened his eyes and wiped sweat from his brow. He looked at me. "Aria, what just happened? What was that?"

I looked at my hands and saw that the different-colored spots were on my skin again. Specs of aqua, green, and purple were all over my body. I shook my head. "I don't know what that was."

I took my eyes off Grayson and saw my mom holding onto my dad and Alexia. Cayne broke my concentration. "Aria, you just channeled both yours and Grayson's powers. You used some of his power to strengthen your own. There is Dark in you and if you don't want to go Dark during the blood moon, you'll need to stop using your Dark powers."

I looked at him with desperation in my eyes. "I don't know what my powers are. I'm not trying to do anything."

Everyone looked at Cayne for an answer but he just rubbed his chin. "All we know for sure is that you have a natural defense power. We have got to test you for different types of powers, but it will not be fun."

My dad shouted, "We will not put her through that!"

Cherise spoke, "Mr. Whitelace, I know that putting Aria through the tests is not ideal, but I agree with my son. There is most definitely some Dark in her and if you all want to keep her Light, she'll need to learn what powers she's capable of."

Cayne added, "The blood moon is fast approaching and with the way things are going, Aria will end up turning Dark."

Grayson's brother looked at me and then back at my parents. "Mr. and Mrs. Whitelace, need I remind you as to what will happen if Aria chooses to join the Dark?."

Alexia huffed, "For God's sake! Instead of all of you bitching and complaining about what may or may not happen, why don't we all let Aria decide what to do? Yes, it is scary. Yes, we will all be affected by her decision, but it is just that. *Her* decision."

The room stayed silent for a moment and I walked towards the window that was on the opposite side of the large room. I looked outside and then turned around to face everyone.

I cleared my throat before I spoke. "Alexia's right. I appreciate you all being concerned for me, but I have decided that I need to go through the tests. I have to know what I'm capable of so I can learn how to control it."

I looked into my mom's eyes. "I know it'll be painful, but it's something I have to do."

My mom's worried stare turned from me to my dad. She spoke softly, "Very well then. We need to make the council aware of what's happening. They need to be involved with all our decisions."

Cherise and Braden smiled at me and then asked my parents, "When would you all like to proceed with the tests?"

My parents looked at each other and then my dad answered. "If possible, tomorrow morning will be fine. We will be present for the entire duration of all the tests."

Cayne interrupted, "Are you sure that's a wise decision, Mr. Whitelace?"d

My dad's face went soft. "Yes. We need to be there to support our daughter. We may add some value to the results of these tests."

Grayson's dad agreed with my dad. "I think that's perfectly reasonable. I think with all of our supervision and help, Aria's tests will be completed smoothly and correctly."

I asked, "What exactly will I have to do?"

Grayson joined me by the large window and held onto my hands while Cayne answered me.

"You will go through some standard blood tests and then go through a series of physical tests. If your council allows you to use our facility, you will be placed in a controlled environment where there will be different obstacles for you to overcome. It usually takes about 6-7 hours for someone to complete it all."

Briar added, "Not many Fae go through the tests, but those who do discover what their powers are almost immediately. After you find out exactly what powers you have, you will be able to better control them."

I nodded and then walked over to my parents. I hugged my mom tightly as my dad put his arms around me. He sighed and then said, "You'll be fine. It'll be painful at times but I have faith in you."

We all stepped apart and looked at the Trebles who were sitting across from us. Mr. Treble looked at his watch and said, "Let's call it a night, shall we? Tomorrow's going to be a very, very long day."

My dad sighed. "You're right. We will call the council on our way home to make sure everything is approved."

Mrs. Treble smiled as she stood up and came over. "Aria, I, like your dad, have a tremendous amount of faith in you. Whatever you decide to choose, know that you will be very powerful and very much loved."

I embraced her as she hugged me and then signaled for her guards to escort us from their home. Grayson walked us out with the guards and as I got into my parent's vehicle, he hugged me and laughed. "Hugs are going all around tonight, huh?"

I laughed with him as I pulled him closer to me. I stayed quiet for a second, taking in his scent. He had a unique, amazing smell. It was a mix of shower gel with freshly picked flowers. It was divine. I stepped away from him and kissed his cheek. "I'll see you in the morning, Treble."

He winked at me as I opened my door. "See you then, Whitelace."

Chapter Twenty-Nine

The next morning our house was chaotic. My parents got the green Light from our council to move forward with the tests for today. Alexia walked into my room as I was finishing up my hair. "Seriously, Aria? Fixing your hair on a day like this? Girl, we've got to get your life-priorities together."

I rolled my eyes as she sat on my bed. "Whatever, Alexia. How does everyone know how painful today will be? The Trebles admitted that not many Fae go through this."

She stood up and walked towards my vanity. She started to play around with my jewelry as she answered me. "They're right. Not many Fae go through the tests, but when they do, it is a recorded event."

She put on one of my silver necklaces that had a butterfly charm on it as she continued on with her story. "From what I can remember reading, a Fae is put in controlled environment, kind of like an arena and they are tested with computer-simulated circumstances."

She walked over to join me near my closet. She lay on the chaise while I finished getting dressed. "The pain that a Fae experiences is a small version of the Reckoning. Each and every time there is a reaction to an event, that Fae goes through the feeling of a Reckoning."

I started to put my shoes on when I looked up at her. "Oh, so the whole soul-being-pulled-from-my-body agony will be felt more than once?"

She sighed. "Well, not necessarily. You'll feel it when a power is activated. If you don't react to certain tests, you won't feel a thing. When you react the computers will be able to tell what powers you have."

I watched her reflection in the mirror of my closet door. "So, it's kind of like an allergy test? I get poked with things and when my body reacts, bam, they know what I'm allergic to."

She rolled her eyes and then laughed. "Yeah, kind of like that."

My mom's voice broke through our conversation. "Girls, are you all ready? Your dad went to check on Declan and he'll be meeting us at the Trebles'."

We both nodded and made our way out of the house.

We were pulling into the driveway when I saw him. Grayson was standing outside of his house, eyes fully lit with that violet color I've started to enjoy seeing.

I got out of the car and rushed over to him. As I got closer to him, I saw that he was upset. His hands were trembling and his eyes were not lit violet with happiness, but with a Dark, frustrated glow behind them.

I kept a couple of feet in between us now. "What's going on? Are you okay?"

He kept his mouth tight for a second and then answered me. "I'm not okay. It's your cousin, Ethan."

My mom walked up to us as Grayson said his name. She asked, "What is it? What's happened with Ethan? Is he okay?"

Grayson was about to answer my mom when his brothers, Cayne and Briar walked outside from the house. Cayne gave us a half-smile. "Good morning, everyone."

Briar looked at us and then at Grayson. "We should all get inside. Things are calming back down."

My family and I walked behind the Trebles as Alexia whispered to me, "Dude, what the hell is going on? Where's Dad?"

We got into the living area and saw my dad was sitting on their large, gray sofa. He stood up, eyes lit blue. "Adalyn, we were wrong. We were so wrong."

My mom rushed over to him. "What happened, Liam? What were we wrong about?"

Cherise and Braden Treble walked into the room. Cherise answered my mom. "What your husband is saying is that we were all wrong about your nephew, Ethan."

My head jerked towards Grayson. I went to stand by his side and grabbed his hand. I mumbled, "What happened?"

Grayson's dad spoke now. "Last night, when you all left we turned in for the evening.

Ethan stayed up in the library. He said he was going to do some research about today's tests and that he'd turn in soon after we did."

Braden took a seat next to his wife and across from my parents. He continued, "This morning I sent our guards to his room, so he could have some breakfast and when they walked in, they noticed that he was missing."

Alexia asked, "Did Violet take him? How did she get in?"

Cherise looked at her husband and then answered my sister. "Violet did not take him. She wouldn't have been able to come near our home without setting off some of our alarms."

I squeezed Grayson's hand tighter and felt the familiar heat radiating from our touch. "Where is Ethan?"

Cayne looked at me, his eyes matching Grayson's glow. "We have reason to believe that your cousin left here to be with his mother again."

I shook my head as the heat from our hands ran up my arm and into my chest. "Are you all sure he's with Violet? If so, why would he ever go back? She was going to kill him."

Cayne's twin, Briar, spoke now. "I—we— don't think that he ever truly left her. We believe that Violet sent him to spy on us."

The heat now filled my entire body. My vision started to get blurry as I heard his voice. "Aria, please, calm down. You're hurting me."

I closed my eyes and took in his scent. His shower gel, the freshly picked flowers. I immediately felt my body start to cool down. I let go of his hand as his guards ran over to him.

I heard one of them ask, "Grayson, sir, are you okay?"

Before I could hear his response, I passed out.

Chapter Thirty

What felt like days later, I woke up on the large, gray sofa in the Trebles' living area. My family and Grayson were hovering over me.

Grayson's Dark, upset glow was gone from his eyes. The violet in them were filled with a bright worry. He leaned down and kissed my forehead. "You scared me, Whitelace."

He helped me sit up, slowly, as my parents handed me a bottle of water.

I took a drink and asked, "What happened? How long was I out?"

Alexia answered me from the other sofa. "You were only out for a couple of minutes. But it was getting a bit scary."

I set the water bottle on the coffee table and sat back. "Wow, really? It feels like I was out for days."

Cherise's voice broke through the others. "Aria, we will get you checked out by our physician, but if you are cleared, we will need to begin the tests right away."

Grayson let his frustration show. "Are you serious, Mother? She just passed out."

My mom responded before Cherise could. "Grayson, thank you for worrying about Aria. However, I agree with your mother. I think that we need to make sure Aria is healthy enough to begin the tests."

Cherise smiled at my mom as she signaled for one of the guards to fetch the doctor.

A few seconds later, a tall, slender man walked into the room. He was wearing a lab coat and greeted everyone in the room. He smiled at me as he introduced himself. When he smiled, I saw that he had a near-perfect smile with the exception of two gold-plated teeth in the back of his mouth.

He spoke, "Hello, Aria, I'm Dr. Brennan. It is a pleasure to meet you. Grayson is constantly talking about you."

I looked at Grayson, who was now blushing. "Come on, doc. Let's not waste everyone's time talking."

Dr. Brennan smiled at me and then signaled for me to open my mouth, so he could take my temperature.

A few minutes after asking me a few questions, he got up from the stool he had been sitting on and smiled at my parents. "You have a very healthy young woman."

He looked back at me. "Aria, if you're feeling up to it, I'll take your blood samples and then you can be taken to the test facility. You've got my green Light to proceed."

Everyone let out a sigh of relief as I nodded at him. He sat back down and took four vials of my blood and then walked out of the room.

Grayson took the doctor's seat and sat next to me. I smiled at him. "So, you're always talking about me, huh?"

He laughed. "Shut it, Whitelace."

He brushed some of the hair that was hanging loose from my pony-tail and looked at me. "Aria, seriously though. Are you ready for today? Are you going to be able to give it 100%?"

I nodded and stood up. I looked around at everyone and asked, "Let's get these tests done, what do you all say?"

My parents hugged each other and smiled at me. Cayne walked towards me. "Very well then. Let's make our way to the test site then."

We all walked through the various hallways in the Trebles' mansion as Alexia finally asked, "Aren't we going to drive to the test site?"

Cherise and Braden laughed as Briar answered her. "Our test site is actually here, on our property. We have a whole wing dedicated to the tests."

My dad moaned, "Oh, wow. That's impressive."

Grayson's family stopped walking as my dad spoke. We stood in front of a pair of wide, black, double doors. Grayson's mom spoke, "These doors lead to the test site. Grayson will walk with Aria to get her set up. The rest of us will be in the viewing room, upstairs."

Alexia huffed, "God, are we going to have to walk another mile to get there?"

Cayne laughed. "Actually, no, we're not. We've got an elevator just around the corner."

Alexia let out a sigh of relief as my parents walked closer to me and hugged me tightly. My mom's eyes were filled with tears as she whispered, "Aria, you'll do great. If and when you feel the Reckoning pain, just remember that it is a temporary thing. It will not last longer than a minute or two"

I nodded and embraced my parents' hug. Grayson cleared his throat. "Aria, are you ready?"

I looked at him and nodded. "Yeah, let's get this over with."

Chapter Thirty-One

After I said my goodbyes to my family and the Trebles, Grayson and I pushed open the heavy doors.

As the doors opened, we were blinded by a bright Light. As I regained my focus I saw that we were standing outside and that it was the sun that was blinding us. I looked around and saw that there was a stream of water on my right and a forest of tall trees to my left.

Grayson interrupted my thought process when he spoke. "Okay, Aria, in a few minutes I will have to exit the premises and you will be alone."

I nodded and stared at a deer that was picking at the tall grass behind the trees on my left. Grayson waved his hand in front of my face. "Aria, pay attention!"

I blushed. "Okay, I'm sorry. You're leaving in a few minutes. What do I do?"

He sighed. "All you'll need to do is explore your surroundings. The tests will happen naturally, and you will feel the Reckoning happen when you've triggered a power."

A horn blared from the sky. Grayson looked up, nodded and then leaned in to hug me. "You'll be fine, babe. I'll be watching from the viewing room."

I squeezed him tighter and took in his familiar scent. The horn blared again and he walked off.

He was about to exit when he turn around and shouted out, "Aria, I love you!"

The doors Grayson exited from slowly started to fade away. He loves me? I love him too, right? Wait, I can't love him!

A loud shriek came from the forest as I was deep in thought. My head jerked to the forest and saw that the deer I was staring at earlier was now floating in the air, being violently shaken.

Immediately I began to run towards the deer to help it, when I crashed into an invisible barrier. I fell back and landed on my rear end.

Damn, that hurt.

What the hell just happened? As I stood up and wiped my hands on my jeans, I saw that the deer's eyes were now glowing violet.

What the hell? How is this possible? I slowly started walking towards the deer again when it noticed me. It stood on its rear legs now and tossed his head violently.

Bright, yellow orbs started flying towards me. I raised my hands to defend myself, when *it* happened.

My neck and arms were jerked back. I shouted out, "Please, stop!"

I felt a fire inside of my chest as my arms and neck were pulled farther back. The burning sensation was throbbing in my heart as the gravity from the earth tried to pull my heart from my chest.

I screamed out, in pain again. A second later, my body was limp on the floor.

Get up, Aria. You can do this.

I forced my wobbly legs up and walked towards the direction of the mysterious deer. This time, I was able to get past the forest line.

The deer's eyes were normal again and it ran further into the forest.

I broke into a jog when I heard screeching coming from the top of the trees. I looked up and saw that there were black crows picking at someone, who was floating in the air.

I focused harder and realized who was crying for help. It was Alexia.

I shouted, "Alexia! I'm coming for you, hold on!"

Alexia's piercing scream nearly deafened me. "Aria, don't! It's a trap! She's here! She's going to kill you!"

I looked around at my surroundings, as I covered my ears from the loud crows. "Who's here?"

Alexia's body flipped around and I saw her eyes were glowing with pain. "Violet is here! She's going to kill you if you come for me!"

I shook my head. "She's not going to kill me, Violet!"

I started to climb one of the trees near me, but could not get a good enough grip to get closer to Alexia.

I yelled, "How did you get up there?"

Alexia cried out, "Violet set me here. You need to get me down, Aria. Please!"

I bit my lip as my nerves started to burn inside of my stomach. I looked up at my sister and raised my hands. Bright, orange orbs flew from my hands and went towards my sister. They surrounded her and started to pull her down.

My body flew into the air and the burning sensation of my heart being ripped from my body was back.

I cried in pain as I closed my eyes and tried to calm myself down.

I opened my eyes after a few seconds and saw that my skin was glowing with different colored spots.

I looked up and saw that my sister was gone and so were the crows.

I shook my head in disbelief and walked deeper into the forest.

I made my way past a herd of grazing deer, when a familiar scent caught my attention.

I saw a boulder with someone sitting on it. It was on top of a grassy hill, and I heard his voice. It was Grayson was crying out in pain. "Aria, come and help me, please!"

Without hesitation, I ran towards him and the boulder and saw him, my love. His eyes were glowing but looked as if they were dimmer than usual.

He whimpered, "If I die, please tell my family that I love them."

Tears started falling from my eyes as I spoke to him. "Grayson, you're not going to die. Quit saying that, please."

He grabbed my hand and I felt the burning sensation of our touch in my palm. He looked into my eyes and I saw that his glow started to get brighter.

I closed my eyes and concentrated on providing him with strength. I was about to open my eyes when I was yanked into the air.

The burning sensation from his touch now filled my entire body. My heart and skull felt as if they were about to explode from the heat at any second.

A few minutes later, I opened my eyes and saw that I was lying on top of the same boulder that Grayson was just on, but he was gone.

How many more tests could I possibly go through? How long had I been here? The test had to be nearly over, right?

I sat on the boulder for a while until I saw the familiar deer in the distance. His sight connected with mine and something in me told me to follow him again.

After an eternity of walking, I noticed that we were now at the stream of water where we had originally started.

I was standing in the same spot that Grayson had left me in. I looked around at my surroundings for my next test when I heard the stream of water turn violent.

Waves were crashing into each other so I ran towards to water's edge. I saw them, my entire family.

My parents were drowning and Declan was holding on to Alexia for dear life.

Declan shouted, "Aria! Help us, please!"

I jumped into the water but was immediately ejected by an invisible force. I tried three more times, but got the same result every time.

My parents continued their struggle for air, when the sun disappeared. I looked up and saw that there was Lightning in the sky.

A second after I noticed the Lightning, rain poured down on me.

Great, that's just what I needed.

Declan and Alexia screamed out, "Aria, hurry!"

I shouted back, "What do I do? I don't know how to help!"

The heavy waves started to pull my siblings into the water when I ran to the water's edge and put my hands in the water.

A bright blue-green orb flew from my palms into the water and a second later, the water was calm again. My body, however, was not.

I floated from the ground, limbs being pulled in different directions. I cried out in pain from the burning sensation that was taking over my body. I looked up towards the sky and saw a blood moon. A second later, I blacked out.

Chapter Thirty-Two

"Aria, you're okay. I'm here, you did it. You're all done."

I slowly opened my eyes and saw Grayson hovering over me. His eyes were glowing, clearly filled with worry.

I tried to reach out to touch him and felt the restraints holding my arms down at my side.

Grayson kissed my forehead and whispered, "It's okay. You're tied down because you were trying to hit everyone when we were helping you out of the test site. You need to rest. Your parents are in the other room."

I closed my eyes and drifted off into a deep sleep.

While I was sleeping, there were no dreams, no thoughts, only Darkness. A peaceful, quiet, worry-free, Darkness.

My mom's troubled voice woke me. "Aria, baby, I'm so sorry you had to go through this."

My dad joined in, "You did amazing, baby. It's all over, we'll be going home soon."

I reached out, and this time, I was able to touch them. The restraints were no longer holding me down.

My mom put her hands on mine and cried, what I think were tears of joy.

Alexia's worried voice came from behind them. "Aria, are you alright?"

I slowly nodded my head as I took a drink of water.

I cleared my throat before I asked, "How long was I in there?"

My parents looked at each other, as my dad reluctantly answered me. "You were only in there for two hours. They're calculating your results now."

Alexia laughed. "You really freaked everyone out. There were people running around, people calling people and people shouting from all corners of the room. It was kidn of funny, until you decided to just pass out."

Before I could give a snarky response, Grayson and his parents walked into the room. Cherise smiled at me. "Aria, I'm glad to see that you're doing well. You're up just in time. Your results are in and finalized. We're going to our meeting room if you all would like to join us?"

My parents looked at me and then at them. Braden smiled, "Of course, Aria, we'll get you a wheelchair. I can only imagine how exhausted your body is."

I smiled, "Thank you."

My dad pushed me down a couple of long hallways and into the enormous meeting room. There were floor to ceiling windows that looked over their backyard.

In the middle of the room, hanging just above the table was a crystal chandelier. Blues, yellows and greens were reflecting from the Light onto the ceiling.

Grayson put his hand on my shoulder and grabbed my attention. "You wanna be next to me, or your parents?"

I smiled at him. "In between you all will be fine."

He blushed and leaned down to kiss me. My dad cleared his throat. "Okay, kids, let's take a seat."

Grayson's dad laughed and sat across from us with the rest of his family.

A team of Dark Fae sat at the end of the table with a bunch of laptops in front of them.

I looked at Grayson, who looked back at me. He gave me a half-smirk and squeezed my hand under the table.

Cherise stood up to introduce us to the men who were going to go over my test results. Grayson interrupted her and asked, "Mom, do you think that you and Dad can go over the results? I don't think we need anyone extra here."

She smiled at us and then looked at her husband. Braden answered him, "Very well then, son."

He escorted the group of men out of the room and thanked them for their time. He walked back over to the meeting table and turned the laptops to face all of us.

Cherise walked over to join her husband at the head of the table, leaving Cayne and Briar sitting alone.

Cayne was tapping a pen on the table while his twin was nervously shaking his leg.

Cherise used her calming voice to start the conversation. "Aria, by now you know that you were in the testing site for less than two hours, am I correct?"

I nodded in agreement as she smiled and continued. "On average, the test has taken most Fae about six to seven hours to complete all the tasks."

I nodded again. I already knew that.

Braden clarified, "Not only does it take them six to seven hours to complete the tasks, but they're in recovery for about one to two weeks."

Cayne whispered, "You're almost fully recovered the same day."

Everyone looked at me as my mom asked, "What does this all mean? Do we know what her powers are?"

Cherise took a deep breath before answering. "Yes, we do."

Her husband pointed at the laptops in front of us and spoke. "Aria reacted to every test that was thrown at her."

I protested, "I only felt the pain a few times, how is that possible?"

Braden walked closer to my parents and I. "You felt the pain when you were supposed to. But you also saw things you weren't supposed to. You heard things that you shouldn't have heard."

I mumbled, "The deer. The crows. The boulder. The water."

Grayson added, "And the blood moon."

Alexia and my parents shrieked. Alexia asked, "Aria, you saw the blood moon?"

She turned her attention to the Trebles as my parents asked, "Was that even a part of her test?"

Cayne answered, "It is the power of foresight. It is technically a part of the test, but almost no one reacts to it."

Cherise added, "Aria passing out was another way her body reacted to the tests."

My dad looked closer at the laptop that was closest to him. His jaw dropped. He stuttered, "Ad-Adalyn, come look at this."

My mom moved in closer and had the same reaction as my dad. My parents asked, "Is this correct? Is this what she is?"

The Trebles looked at each other, and then at my parents, who then turned to me. "Yes, it is one hundred percent accurate. There is no question as to Aria's nature."

Grayson squeezed my hand as Alexia asked, "Well? What is it?"

My parents kept their focus on me as Cayne answered from across the table. "Aria is in fact, a true natural."

Chapter Thirty-Three

Grayson let go of my hand and asked, "Are you sure? How is this possible? What do we do now?"

I asked him, "You didn't know the results already?"

He shook his head. "No, I didn't want to know. I told them I'd wait to find out with you."

Cherise and Braden sat back down across from us. She spoke, "Well, I'm sure that the Light council would like to be made aware of this."

My mom agreed. "Yes, they will want to know."

Braden added, "There's not much we can do except wait until the blood moon. Aria will have to choose in just nine days."

Alexia squeezed my free hand and asked, "Aria, your Reckoning will not be the same as any of ours. Are you okay?"

I looked around at the other people in the room before I answered her. "I don't know. I don't know what I'm going to do."

My mom gasped. "Aria, you do know that if you choose Dark you will no longer be a member of this family, right?"

Grayson demanded, "And you do know that if you go Light, we will never be able to truly love one another, right?"

Tears were running down my face and my hands were shaking. I pulled them from free from Alexia and Grayson.

I cried out, "Why does this have to happen to me? Why do I have to be a natural-born? Why do I have to choose Light or Dark?"

My mom walked over to me and put her arms around me. "I know this is hard, baby. But it's just the way of our kind. Everything happens for a reason."

I pulled away from her embrace. "Why do we have to choose? What will happen if I don't choose a side?"

Everyone stayed quiet for a couple of seconds. In true Cayne form, he broke the silence. "Aria, the blood moon will choose for you, if you refuse to make a choice on your own."

I shook my head, "No, that's crap! I want to be with Grayson, but I want my family. Can't I have both?"

My dad walked over to me as Cherise spoke. "I'm sorry, Aria. I don't think that's an option."

Braden chimed in, "If you choose Light, it doesn't mean you and Grayson can't be friends. It just means you all will not be able to date anymore."

Grayson stood up next to me. "No one will tell Aria and I what we can do or who we can date."

His parents sighed while his brother, Briar, responded. "Don't be foolish, brother. You know it is a firm law."

I answered Briar before Grayson could. "Laws are sometimes meant to be broken or changed."

Chaos broke through the room. My dad shouted at me, "Aria, you will not talk about breaking Fae law!"

Alexia added, "Aria, that is a punishable offense!"

I slammed my hands down on the table and demanded silence. "I'm not a teenager who is throwing a tantrum. I am a young woman who will not be controlled! I will do whatever I want! I am not going through a Reckoning and that is a natural Fae thing, so I'm already breaking tradition, right?"

Grayson smiled at me and looked at the others for confirmation. Cayne quietly responded to me. "Spoken like a true natural-born leader."

His parents glared at him as his twin continued. "I agree. Aria, you are a force to be reckoned with. You have got my support with whatever you decide."

Alexia stood at my side. "I don't agree with everything you're saying, but I love you. I trust that you'll make the best decision for you."

Grayson's parents stood next to my parents with a dumbfounded expression. They all looked at us with disapproval in their eyes. The Trebles' eyes were lit up with their now-normal, violet color, while my parent's eyes lit up with the blue I've grown up with.

My mom broke the tense silence. "Aria, Alexia, we need to go home now. The blood moon is in nine days and we obviously have a lot to go over before then."

I looked at my parents and for some reason, I laughed. "I'm not going home with you all. The Trebles have gone out of their way to help us. Hell, they've moved mountains to help me."

My dad's eyes lit up a little brighter. "Aria, do not speak to us like this. Say your goodbyes and meet us in the car."

Grayson tried to get me to reason with him when I felt something strange happen. I felt my eyes twitch a bit. I looked at my reflection in a mirror that was hanging on the wall and saw that my eyes were glowing with a mixture of violet and blue.

I didn't let my worry show as I pulled my shoulders back and spoke. "I will go home, when and if I'm ready. Now, you all can go ahead and leave."

Chapter Thirty-Four

The expressions on my parents faces as they left will be engraved in my memory forever. As Grayson walked them out of the house, Cayne walked over to me. "Aria, are you alright?"

I nodded as he asked, "Are you sure? I know that you didn't want your parents to see you stressed, but I can tell something isn't right."

I looked at myself in the mirror again and saw that my eyes were still glowing, just not as bright now.

Cayne pushed on, "Aria, I know you're going through a lot of emotions right now. Just try to keep control of them. Now that we know that you're a natural-born, we will need to keep track and monitor the different things that happen to you, leading up until the blood moon."

I nodded in agreement, still not talking. Grayson walked back into the meeting room. He was instantly by my side. "Your parents will be fine. They'll forgive you for tonight."

I huffed. "I don't care if they do, or not."

He put his arm on my shoulder. "Don't say that, babe. I know you care. I know that you've just been through a lot today. Hell, I don't know how you're not still sitting in the wheelchair."

I turned around to hug him and my emotions took over. I started shaking and crying. "Why is all of this happening to me? Why can't I just be normal?"

Grayson squeezed me tighter and whispered to me. "You don't want to be normal. Normal is boring, and you, babe, are far from boring."

I let out a giggle while trying to recompose myself. "I hate this. I'm an emotional wreck. Mundanes talk about how their hormones are always out of whack. I'd hate to see them go through what we have to go through."

Cayne laughed from across the room. "Yeah, the world would probably be a much scarier place if Mundane girls went through what Fae do."

I stayed the night at Grayson's and woke up to my phone ringing loudly. I looked at the time before picking it up.

Two in the afternoon? I must have been exhausted.

I answered the anonymous phone call. "H-hello?"

I yawned as the person on the other side of the phone stayed quiet.

"Hello? Who is this? Who are you looking for?"

A lady's voice broke through the phone. "Hello, Aria. It's your aunt, Violet."

Chills went up and down my spine as I shot out of bed. She laughed as if she could hear me. "My dear, dear, niece. Did you actually think that my own son would betray me? Were you really, truly that naive?"

I stayed quiet as I started to get dressed in a frenzy. Violet's voice broke the silence. "Well? Are you going to ignore your aunt? I'm pretty sure my sister raised you better than that."

I put my hair in a ponytail and left the room to look for Grayson. I spat out, "I'm not naive, I just thought Ethan was sick of living with a psycho like you."

She let out a strained laugh as I bumped into Cayne in the hallway. I pointed at the phone and mouthed, "It's Violet."

His eyes widened and he proceeded to text someone on his cellphone. Violet cleared her throat. "Oh, Aria, there's no need for name calling. Anyways, I hear that you'll be choosing a side in a few days, during the blood moon if my information is correct?"

I stayed mute as she went on. "Sebastian thinks it'd be a wonderful idea if we were able to attend your unique Reckoning. He is after all, the one true Fae."

My jaw tightened at the thought of seeing Violet with Sebastian. Grayson and Briar ran up to Cayne and I, who were now sitting in one of the spare rooms. All the Treble brother's eyes were brightly lit. I glanced at myself in a nearby mirror and saw that my eyes were not.

Violet's annoyed voice came through the phone again. "Hello, Aria? Are you still there?"

I let out a simple, "Yes."

She chuckled. "Oh, wonderful. So will you be inviting Sebastian and I to your little blood moon Reckoning?"

Instead of asking her question, I blurted out, "Sebastian is not the one true Fae. Have you all forgotten about Camila? Ask him, has he forgotten about his wife?"

The line crackled with her rage as she said, "Camila is no longer alive. She is not the true Fae. She is, I mean was, a Light Fae."

I laughed now. "Oh, my dear aunt. You seem to have skipped Fae history 101. Camila has not been seen in a long time, but that doesn't make her dead. If that were the case, many people would say that Sebastian was dead. Camila, along with Sebastian, is an original Fae. She is the reason we all exist."

My aunt's anger was growing. "Camila is not alive! Sebastian's bravery to become the first natural, Dark Fae makes him the one and only absolutely original Fae."

I sighed. "Okay, Violet. Whatever you say. I guess we'll all learn the truth, one day, right?"

Violet stayed quiet, so I went on, "As for the invitation to my Reckoning, I wouldn't suggest you or Sebastian show up. I don't think either of you would like to be around me when my powers come full force. Your coward of a son should be able to tell you that some of my powers are already stronger than yours."

She sounded disgusted with me as she responded. "My son is no coward. He has told me of your kiddie-powers and I find them quite cute. You have a natural defense power? That's adorable. I have not met a natural defense Fae that I haven't been able to break down."

I laughed out loud now. Grayson's eyes widened at my reaction. "Violet, had your son stayed around a bit longer, he'd be able to tell you that I am a natural-born with all the true powers. I do not have to kill anyone to gain my power, and that should scare you and Sebastian."

With that, Violet ended the phone call. I set the phone down on the wooden desk and looked up at the Treble brothers, their eyes still lit up by that beautiful purple color.

Grayson smiled at me. "You're a badass, Whitelace."

Cayne and Briar laughed together. Cayne threw a pillow at me. "You're going to be someone to be reckoned with, girl."

Mrs. Treble broke up our laughter as she walked into the room. "Good afternoon everyone. I'm glad you all have gotten your rest."

She looked at me now. "Aria, your family is downstairs. They wish to speak with you."

I looked at Grayson and then let out a long sigh. "Alright, let's get this over with."

Cherise smiled at me and put her hand on my shoulder as I approached the door. "Be gentle with your words. I know you're feeling a ton of emotions right now, but so are they. Your parents are good people."

I returned the smile and nodded as I walked out of the room and down the spiral stairs.

I walked into the living area and saw that my parents were standing by the large windows, staring outside. My heart warmed as I saw my dad rubbing my mom's back.

I greeted them. "Hi, Mom and Dad."

They turned and gave me a weak smile. My mom spoke first. "You look well rested, baby."

My dad added, "How are you feeling?"

I walked closer to them and sat on the sofa. "I slept a lot last night. I'm feeling better."

My parents left the window and took the sofa across from me. I looked at them, wondering why they had come.

They looked like they were waiting for an apology so I crossed my hands in front of my chest.

My mom mirrored my stance as my dad spoke. "Aria, last night was a bit strange."

I crossed my legs now and started to tap my foot, ready to spring up in protest.

He continued, "We're not here to argue with you, baby. We just came to tell you that we're sorry. We're sorry we over-reacted. We're just so scared for you."

My mom uncrossed her hands and spoke a little more assertively, "We know that you are going to make the right decision during the blood moon."

I looked at her and then uncrossed my legs and arms. "I know that you all are scared, but how do you think that I feel about all of this? I didn't ask for any of it. I thought I'd grow up, go through my Reckoning and be normal like Alexia."

My dad moved to sit next to me. He put his arm around me and squeezed my body close to his. "I'm sorry that you have to go through this, too. We just want you to know that you're not alone. I know that it sucks having to choose the Light or Dark, but I agree with what the Trebles said last night. If you choose Light, it doesn't mean you won't be able to talk to Grayson anymore. You all just can't be romantically together."

I pulled away from him a little and looked into his eyes. "Why can't I? I know you all think this is just some form of puppy love, but it's not. It is something stronger than that."

Before I could say anything else, Grayson walked into the room and finished it for me. "Mr. and Mrs. Whitelace, what we have is one hundred percent love for each other."

My mom gasped a little as he walked closer to us. "I don't know if you all know or not, but when Aria and I touch, we feel the destructive fire. Not the fire exactly, but we feel the sparks that the two original Fae felt."

My parents both leaped to their feet as he said this. My mom cried out. "How do you all know about the destructive fire?"

My dad added, "Are you sure that is what you two are experiencing? If it is, you both know how those stories end, right?"

I looked at my parents and felt the tingling sensation in my eye sockets. My eyes were glowing bright violet and blue now.

I spoke slowly, "The only thing we are sure about is that we're supposed to be together. Fate brought us together and we are both aware of how the other Faes' stories ended up."

Grayson grabbed my hand and the burning sparks shot through my body. He added, "The others are not us and we are not them. I am Grayson and she is Aria."

Cayne walked into the room with his mom when Grayson and I let go of each other's hand. Cayne tilted his head. "Is everything okay here?"

Grayson nodded and took the seat next to me. My dad moved back to my mom's side so Mrs. Treble could sit with us.

Cherise smiled at all of us. "I'm sorry Braden couldn't be here with us today. He's got some things to take care of with our guards. Ethan shouldn't have been able to leave these premises undetected."

Cayne continued his mom's sentence. "My dad is a little concerned with our home's security. He has sent me in his place."

My parents nodded together, smiling at the Trebles. Grayson asked, "Where do you all think will be the best place for Aria to go through her Reckoning?"

My dad spoke without hesitating. "We believe it's best if Aria goes through her Reckoning at the Light's council chambers."

Cayne questioned, "Didn't Violet burn down your council's chambers?"

My mom nodded. "Yes, she did. We do have a new council location. We also have an interim council leader."

My dad stood up. "That's part of the reason we're here."

He looked at Mrs. Treble. "I am the Light council leader until Lucas is found."

Chapter Thirty-Five

I stood by my dad's side. "Dad! That's great, I'm so happy for you!"

My mom hugged us and as I pulled away from my parent's embrace I saw Grayson was staring at me from his seat.

His mother spoke in her calm tone. "Congratulations, Mr. Whitelace. I hope you understand, this somewhat changes our relationship."

My dad smiled at her. "I am very aware of that. That is why I wanted to come tell your family in person. I appreciate the way you've welcomed us into your home with open arms."

I looked at my parents and at Mrs. Treble with confusion. I asked, "Dad, what's going on?"

My mom answered for him. "Because of our status as head family of the Light, we are no longer able to come to Mr. and Mrs. Treble's home. We also had to tell you that your romantic relationship with Grayson must come to an end, today."

I protested, "The hell it does! You all just said I had until my Reckoning to see and be with Grayson!"

I threw my hands up and saw that my skin turned bright blues and greens again.

My mom's eyes lit up with fury and shouted back, "You will not disrespect us again, young lady. You're coming home with us, now!"

She put her hand on my arm and went flying back.

My dad's eyes were lit up now and yelled at me. "Aria Whitelace! You must stop this!"

He did the same as my mom had just done and ended up flying across the room. My eyes were glowing so brightly I could see the violet and blue radiating off the near-white walls.

My dad was helping my mom back up when Grayson stood in between us. He held his hands out at the three of us as Cayne spoke.

"Aria, please, calm down. They are your parents."

Cherise's guards were in the room now and were surrounding her, protecting her, I'm sure.

I looked at all of them and set my hands back down at my sides. I spoke with a strained voice. "Mom, Dad, I love you but you all need to leave."

My dad stood in front of my mom, on the defense now and let out a snarl. "You're coming home with us!"

I rolled my eyes and felt a fire leap from my chest into my arms and out of my hands. A bright orange orb flew at my parents. My dad lifted his hands and an invisible force knocked the orb to the wall next to him.

Frustrated, I lifted my hands again and threw another orb at him. I screamed out, "You all will leave, now!"

He dodged my orb and threw my mom behind the sofa for protection. My mom lifted her arms and a bright yellow orb came flying at me. I laughed as it hit a barrier and dissipated.

My mom shouted, "Aria, what are you thinking? Why are you attacking us?"

My eyes were burning my skull from their bright glow when I yelled out, "I do not want to see you all until my Reckoning. I will send word to you all when I decide on a location."

I lifted my arms and felt a strong invisible presence in my palms. I glanced at the windows as they opened on their own and then I threw my hands at my parents who went flying out of the window.

The second my parents were out of the house, the windows slammed shut. I put my hands by my side and walked over to the window. I saw my parents standing beside their car, surrounded by Light Fae guards.

I closed the blinds and turned around to face the Trebles who were all staring at me in disbelief.

Grayson was about to walk towards me when I raised my hand to stop him. "Don't come near me. I don't want to hurt you."

Cherise pushed one of her guards out of her way. "Aria, you'll only hurt him if you want to hurt him. You didn't want to hurt your parents, but you did want to scare them. I'm pretty sure you did just that."

Cayne spoke now, "Aria, what you just did was amazing to watch. It is a bit scary, but it was amazing. I'm proud that you're obviously learning how to use your powers."

I collapsed onto the chaise next to me. "I guess I am. I knew exactly what I wanted to do. I didn't see what threw my parents out of the house, but I could feel it. I was holding on to something that wrapped them up and set them outside."

Cherise took a seat on the sofa that was closest to me. "You are an amazing young woman. Whatever you decide, Light or Dark, you will be an amazing asset to the family."

She looked back at her guards. "Fetch my husband. He needs to be made aware of the situation at hand."

The tallest, Dark man nodded his head and exited the room. Mrs. Treble looked back at me, while signaling for her boys to sit down. "Aria, have you given the location for your Reckoning any thought? It will be a very powerful night and if you choose the correct location, it will enhance your powers tremendously."

Cayne coughed. "That's a bit scary."

Grayson smiled at me as he slowly put his hand on mine. His scent calmed me down immediately. The Light from my eyes went from an angry fire to a healing glow.

His soothing voice broke my concentration. "I think I know where we need to go. It might help keep you calm."

He looked at Cayne, who was smiling from ear to ear. Cayne added, "I agree. I think you all should go there this evening."

Cherise was about to question us when Mr. Treble walked into the room. "Is everyone okay? The guards told me it's urgent news?"

Mrs. Treble assured her husband. "We are all okay but yes, it is most definitely an urgent matter."

She looked at me. "Aria, would you like to tell my husband what just happened, or shall I?"

I took a deep breath and started to go over everything that had just happened.

Mr. Treble was in shock when he found out that my parents were the ruling family of the Light Fae. He agreed that it'd be best if Grayson and I got away from the house for the evening, as long as we took guards with us.

Chapter Thirty-Six

Grayson and I reluctantly agreed to his dad's terms and left in one of their SUVs.

As we pulled up to our grassy hill by the lake, my nerves started to go crazy. I blushed as Grayson rushed over to open my door for me.

He gave me a half-smirk as I took his hand. "Right this way, Ms. Whitelace."

We walked towards the hill that had a nook, but instead of going inside, we climbed to the top of the hill.

Grayson laid out a red striped blanket and we sat next to each other.

I sat down and got comfortable as he ran to the car for something. I lay on my back and stared up at the starry sky. I was lost in thought when Grayson came back.

He cleared his throat so I'd turn my attention to him. He smiled and held out a basket that was packed with food.

I returned the smile. "What's all that, Mr. Treble?"

He set it down and sat down next to me. "It's a homemade dinner. I didn't cook it because that would have just been horrifying, but I did have someone cook it for us."

I got up so I could lean back on my elbows while he served me some diet soda. He handed me my glass as he asked, "How are you doing, Aria?"

I took a drink of my cold soda and then sat up. "I'm okay. Why do you ask?"

He shook his head and scooted closer to me. "That's not what I mean. I know you're okay right now, but how are you dealing with everything? Your parents, Ethan, Violet, your Reckoning."

I let out a long sigh. "I don't know Grayson. Don't you ever sometimes think that being normal wouldn't be such a bad thing? We'd be able to be together, there would be no

Light or Dark fighting and there would be no Reckoning."

He put his hand under my chin. "The grass isn't always greener on the other side, babe."

I looked into his eyes as he continued, "I know the whole Reckoning thing sucks, and I can't imagine how you're feeling about your aunt, but you've got me. You've got your parents. We all love you."

I stayed looking into his eyes, getting myself lost for a couple of seconds. He loves me. He hasn't told me that since he walked out of my testing site.

He put his other hand on my face and squeezed my cheeks together. "Aria, I love you. I will love you no matter what you decide to do."

My eyes started to glow with a bright and burning desire. "I love you too, Grayson."

He leaned in to kiss me and when our lips touched, we were lost in each other. The burning sensation that we felt when our hands touched wasn't nearly as powerful as what we were experiencing now.

His passion and love for me translated clearly in his kiss. I felt as though my heart leaped out of my chest and went into his.

I slowly pulled away from him and saw that he was short of breath. I whispered, "Grayson, you will forever have my heart."

He opened his eyes before responding to me. "And you will forever have mine."

Grayson and I spent the next few days at our secret hideout, while Cayne brought us food and supplies since he was the only person, other than the guards, who knew where it was.

I got out of bed and started to cook breakfast when Grayson grabbed my waist from behind. "Good morning, love."

I kissed him. "Morning. It was nice of Cayne to bring us groceries yesterday."

He smiled at me. "Yeah, for sure. Um, Aria, I told my mom that we'd be going home today."

I turned back around to face him. "Do we have to?"

He put his pajama pants on, over his Dark gray boxers, then he took a seat at the kitchen table. "Yeah, we need to. Aria, the blood moon is happening in two days. You still haven't told your parents where you'll go for your Reckoning and they're insisting we tell them today."

I turned my back to him so I could continue to cook. "I'll call Alexia later so she can tell them where the Reckoning will be."

Grayson's voice perked up. "Oh, you have decided on a location?"

I cracked an egg into the red skillet pan before answering him. "Yup, I sure have."

I heard him get out of the chair and walk towards me. He stood next to me and turned on the coffee machine. "So, where's it going to happen?"

I drizzled some cheese into the pan and without looking at him I said, "My Reckoning will happen here."

He set down two coffee cups and stayed quiet. I could practically hear his heart jumping out of his chest. "Aria, this is our spot. Only Cayne knows where we're at. Are you sure you want everyone here? My family and yours?"

I grabbed two plates from the cabinet over the sink and started to serve our food. "Yeah, I think this will be the best place for it to happen. At the top of the hill to be a bit more exact."

Grayson smiled at me, pulled me close to him and then passionately kissed me.

We finally stopped kissing when he smiled at me. "Very well then, Aria. I'll notify my family and we will stay here until the Reckoning."

My eyes immediately started to glow with happiness as I hugged him.

I walked to the small room where we slept and got my cellphone. I sent a text to Alexia. "Hey, I'm okay. Here are the coordinates for where the Reckoning will be. Please tell Mom and Dad for me. See you in a couple of days. Love you."

Chapter Thirty-Seven

The next day went by pretty quickly as all of the Trebles were in and out preparing the outside of our hideaway for my Reckoning.

The grassy hill top had white lace that ran from the top of it towards two different groups of chairs.

The set-up was similar to a wedding as one side was clearly set up for my family, while the other side was for the Trebles.

On my family's side the lace was tinted a bright blue with silver chairs. Grayson's family also had silver chairs but the lace that surrounded them was a beautiful violet.

I stood atop the hill, staring at everyone running around when I heard Grayson walk up behind me.

"Hey, Aria. You ready for tonight?"

He signaled for me to sit on the grass with him.

"Yeah, I guess. I'm ready to get all of this behind me."

He put his arm around my shoulder. "Do you know what you're going to choose?"

I could feel his nerves running wild. I leaned my head on his shoulder. "I actually don't know. I'll just pick what feels right in the moment. It helps that I won't have to say a scripture of any kind."

He laughed. "You were doing so good when we were teaching you those."

I elbowed him. "Yeah, yeah, yeah. I'm just glad that I don't have to actually memorize them anymore. I feel like I would have totally botched either one of them."

Grayson laughed as a number of black SUVs pulled up. I stood back up with his help. He grabbed my hand. "Looks like your parents are here."

I rolled my eyes, annoyed. "Seriously? Is the parade necessary?"

He started to follow me down the hill. "Aria, they are the Light Fae leaders. It is necessary for their protection."

I sighed. "Yeah, I guess you're right. It's just going to take some time to get used to it."

I stood in front of the SUVs as some Light Fae guards opened the doors. Alexia and Declan were the first of my family members to exit the vehicles.

Declan ran towards me. "Aria! I've missed you so much!"

I hugged him and squeezed him tightly. "I know, I can't believe I'm going to say this, but I missed you too, short stuff."

Alexia stood a couple of feet away from me, next to Cayne.

She smiled at me as I ended the hug with Declan. She waved at me. "Hey biatch. You're looking good. Did you get a stylist for this or what?"

I was wearing a long, white dress with a headband of freshly picked flowers. I had on some designer leather heels and lifted my dress so my shallow sister could see them. "No, I actually picked out this outfit on my own."

She walked around me to get a view of the entire outfit. She whistled. "Not bad, girl. Not bad at all."

I walked closer to her. "Shut up and give me a hug."

Alexia hugged me tightly as I whispered, "Where are Mom and Dad?"

She let go of me and looked back at the SUVs. "They're still in the car. They're on a phone conference but will be done soon."

As if on cue, the SUV doors opened again. My mom was helped out of the vehicle as my dad followed suit. My parents looked at the grassy hill and my mom's eyes were immediately filled with tears.

I walked towards them as my mom ran towards me with open arms. She wrapped her arms around me and just cried. "Aria, baby. I love you so, so much. I hope you know that."

Tears threatened to fall from my eyes as I nodded in agreement. I whimpered, "I love you, too. I love you all so much."

My dad's arms were around the pair of us as Cayne cleared his throat. "Excuse me, Mr. and Mrs. Whitelace. My parents would like to show you all around before we begin with Aria's Reckoning."

My parents were hesitant to let me go, but they kissed my forehead and agreed to go on the quick tour with Cayne.

I took a deep breath and held onto Grayson's hand for reassurance. "Everything is going to be okay, right?"

He grabbed my other hand and stood directly in front of me. "Everything will be fine. You will choose what you were destined to."

I kissed him and headed back to the top of the grassy hill.

The sun quickly disappeared as everyone took their seats at the bottom of the hill. As I looked down one last time, I saw blue and purple glowing eyes staring back at me.

Just as we were all waiting silently for the blood moon to appear, it happened. Violet's laughter rang all around us. She had arrived.

Chapter Thirty-Eight

I stood up and saw her walking towards the seating area. She had her palms up and was clearly pushing through both Light and Dark guards.

She shouted, "You all didn't think you could keep me from witnessing this, did you?"

No one answered as she got closer to the people I loved. A couple of feet behind her, I noticed that Ethan was walking towards everyone with a deadly grin spread across his face.

I felt the familiar angry heat take over my body. I looked at my arms and saw that my skin had filled with greens and blues. I felt the glow of my mixed eyes radiating.

Violet must have seen them too, because she immediately stopped walking.

I laughed now. "The two of you have a lot of nerve coming here."

Ethan winced. "Cousin, you couldn't think I'd actually leave my mother's side. You are a fool!"

I threw my hands up as rain started to pour down on all of us. "Why would you want to trick us? What did you get out of it?"

My cousin stood next to his mom now. "I couldn't track you because of your natural defenses, so I had to get close to you. You had to trust me so those defenses against me would weaken."

Violet swayed her arm from left to right. "Hence, the reason we are here. Ethan was able to track you down very easily tonight."

The Dark and Light guards had recovered and were now surrounding my family and the Trebles.

The rain was not just a soft drizzle as I felt a tug in my chest. I looked at the sky and saw that the moon was starting to slowly make its way from out the clouds.

I turned my attention back to my loved ones and then at Violet and saw that they all had their eyes glowing.

Violet raised her hands as if to signal that she surrendered. "I'm just here for the Reckoning. I will not harm anyone or interfere in any way."

Before I could respond, the tugging in my chest pulled me down to the ground.

I heard my mom's voice shout out. "Guards, surround the hill! It is beginning!"

The burning sensation that I felt during the tests could not have prepared me for this. My entire body felt as if it were being pulled in every direction.

I screamed out for mercy. "Please, Grayson, make it stop!"

No one came to help me. There was only Darkness. I could feel myself passing out from the pain, but suddenly my body was pulled into the air.

I opened my eyes and saw that the blood moon was just above me. It had broken through the clouds and was shining its Dark Light onto me.

Every bone in my body was cracking and I felt as if my insides were being ripped out.

I heard Grayson's voice inside my head. "Aria, remember, when you feel the worst, it is time for you to claim a side. Only declare your choice when you feel like the pain cannot get any worse."

I felt the burning take over my body now. My skin started to boil up as I let my body go limp so I could concentrate.

My pain quickly turned into anger when I heard everyone's opinions run through my memory.

Aria, do what's best for you. Choose what you were destined for. If you choose Light, you will lose him. If you choose Dark, you will lose us.

I lifted my hands and felt an energy pulsating in my palms. I opened my eyes and saw that a large, clear orb was forming in my hands.

My eyes radiated frustration from my sockets as I looked up at the moon. "I damn you, blood moon. I damn you! I have made my decision!"

The silence was deafening. "I do not choose Light."

I heard Violet's laughter fill the silent void.

I continued, "I do not choose the Dark either. I choose myself!"

I let the clear orb fly from my palms, towards the sky and then it was done. My body fell to the ground as I drifted off into Darkness.

Chapter Thirty-Nine

What have I done? Where am I? Am I alive?

No one answered my questioning mind but a blinding Light flooded the room I was now laying in.

I looked around at my surroundings and saw that I was in an all-white room. Every piece of furniture was white lined with gold trimmings.

I sighed. "Oh God, is this like, heaven?"

A woman's soft voice came from behind the wall. "No, my sweet child. This is not heaven, but you are safe."

I walked around the corner and saw a woman was sitting at a large kitchen table.

She was wearing a long, gold gown that complemented her matching hair. Her eyes were the perfect shade of blue. She smiled at me and gestured for me to take a seat next to her.

I walked towards her and was surprised with how comfortable I felt with her.

She took a bite of her salad as she spoke to me. "Aria Whitelace, I'm sure you're wondering who I am and why you're here."

I nodded as a mundane man brought me a salad and a drink. I took a sip of the water as she continued. "Well, first of all, my name is Camila Harper."

I spit out the water. "Oh! Um, I'm sorry."

She laughed, showing off her perfectly straight teeth. "Don't worry about it. We'll have someone clean it up. And to be honest, I'd be a bit worried if you did not react to my name."

I took another quick drink of my ice-cold water and started to eat my salad. I asked, "Why am I here? Where are we?"

Camila set down her salad fork. "We're at a place I created called Zion."

I looked at her, confused. "Zion? Where is that?"

She took a drink of her red wine. "Zion is in between earth and heaven. It is a safe place for strong Fae. I created my new home when my husband Sebastian created the Dark Fae. I have been waiting here for someone like you."

I asked, "Someone like me?"

She stood up and moved closer to me. She grabbed my hand and looked into my eyes. "Child, you are the bravest Fae of all time. What you did tonight, choosing yourself is one of the bravest things any Fae has done."

She sat in the chair closest to me. "You have just changed the way our world works forever."

I pushed my salad plate aside. "How is that possible? I just remember passing out."

She set her free hand on our grip. "You denied the Light and Dark side. You, my dear, are the first of your kind."

I shook my head. "I'm not the first of any kind."

She stood up and I followed her over to a mirror that was hanging in the dining room.

"Look deep into your soul, you'll know exactly what you are."

I looked at my reflection and saw what she was talking about. I jumped back. "How do I have three colors in my eyes? They should be either violet or blue."

She made a clicking sound with her mouth. "No, no, no. Because of you, Fae will have the choice not to choose a side. You are both. You are a Dark Fae and you are Light."

My eyes lit up in surprise. "What do you mean I am both? How is that even possible?"

"All things are possible in this world. You should know that by now."

I leaned towards the mirror and looked at the swirling colors of gray, blue and violet in them. I put my right hand on my cheek. "What will I tell my parents? Will I be able to be with Grayson still?"

"That is entirely up to you. Do you want to be with him? Do truly love him, or are you in love with the idea of him?"

I put my hand down and turned away from the mirror. "I love Grayson and my family. Because I'm neither Light or Dark, can I choose to be with both?"

Camila looked at me with interest in her eyes. "To be honest Aria, I am not sure. This has never happened before. Why don't you stay with me, here in Zion, until we can sort it out?"

"What about my family? They'll all be worried about me. They'll think I'm dead."

She stared at a book on the table for a second and then asked, "What if there was a way that we could assure them that you are safe?"

"How would we do that?"

"I have a few different ways we can send messages to them. You can go to them in their dreams and let them know what you are doing here."

I asked, "Don't you think that would worry them even more? They'll think they're losing their minds or something."

She shook her head. "Not exactly. I can join you in their dreams. They'll know you are safe if you are with me."

"Okay, but if I don't get back soon, what will we do about Violet and Sebastian? Surely they wont wait for me to get back to continue with their plans."

"I agree, that's why it is important that we get things going very quickly. Why don't you get some rest and we can begin when you wake up?"

I let out a long yawn. "Yeah, you're probably right. Sleep sounds really good about now."

She guided me to a room that was filled with white décor and bedding. "This can be your room. I hope you find it comfortable."

She left the bedroom and I quickly undressed. I jumped into the bed and it felt as though it were made out of feathers. I closed my glowing eyes and for the first time, in a long time, I fell asleep peacefully."

Want more from this author?

Check out all of Abel Ozuna's projects on
http://abelozuna.com

Follow Abel Ozuna:

Newsletter: http://abelnewsletter.com

Twitter: http://twitter.com/abelozuna4

Facebook: http://facebook.com/abelozuna04

Join his newsletter: http://abelnewsletter.com